MURDER IN COTTISTHORPE

KEITH S. THOMSON

THOMSON PRODUCTIONS

This book is dedicated to my wife of 60 years, Linda Price Thomson, with gratitude for her love and support. And to my daughters Jessica and Elizabeth who so strongly encouraged the work on this project.

PROLOGUE

Difficult to see in the half-light. A musty smell of old paint and wood. Across the dark space a man waited for him; a stranger whose face was hidden, standing silently – awkwardly – with large hands held forward. Neither spoke. The stranger tried to slip past, to the door behind. He had to be stopped. Philip grabbed for him; held him by the throat. Even close up the stranger had no face, but he called out – screamed almost. Philip's hands tightened on his throat. The screams went on until his head was smashed against the wall; against the musty-smelling wooden wall. Screaming, hitting, holding tighter. Then it stopped.

It almost seemed he'd had this dream before. So often that he was half sure it was true. But he never knew who he had killed, or why. But then he did – find out what it meant, that is.

CHAPTER 1

If anything can be said to have started at a given time or place, his life changed because of the 8:30 am train from Philadelphia to New York, on May 20, 1988. Of course, it might have all happened anyway, but who can know? Were the events of the next three months just like the tree that philosophers talk about, falling in the forest? The tree was going to fall anyway, and the only question was whether anyone would see or hear it. Probably it was more of a question of whether or not he pushed the mixed-metaphorical tree. Sooner or later, he would have gone back to Cottisthorpe.

On that particular morning, he had been dozing, looking out of the window but only half noticing what was outside. It was a gray and overcast morning. Humid: quite a nasty day really, a portent of the summer days to come. He was tired of his job, of the pressure, and of too many over-anxious meetings with his staff. Now he was going to a meeting with the New York office, which would probably make things worse.

Philip Jerome Kennedy Halliday was, on that particular day, an investment banker. A pretty good one; maybe not great, but his last annual bonus had been in the high, the very high, six figures and his small office in Philadelphia was reckoned to be one of the rising success stories for the main company on Wall Street. Philip was British – you can always tell the Brits by their triple initials – the staff called him PJ, however, to his face at least. He wasn't sure what they called him behind his back but guessed it was not wholly complimentary.

The trouble was, making money in the financial world had turned out to be extremely hard work, especially for someone like him. By undergraduate training at Durham University in England, a Harvard MBA, and by bent of personality, Philip was an historian. So when he looked at market performance he expected it to proceed in some quasi-orderly fashion according to an historical pattern. None of that seemed to work anymore. The past year had worn all their nerves pretty thin. No one knew whether last year's crash (October 1987) was a one-time blip or the beginning of a downward trend in an over-valued market. Making money, it was clear, was becoming a very costly business – in terms of people, computers, data, and sheer mental energy. Philip was bushed. His people probably knew it, but it was still only slowly dawning on him that they needed a different boss.

Just less than six feet tall, Halliday usually dressed in

bankers' gray suits, his only daring bit of color being a collection of stylish ties. For the weekends he had sports jackets (English tweed) and blazers. He didn't own any jeans. Women found him mildly attractive but a bit stiff. Which he didn't quite know how to change. He hated dancing and popular music; loved the classics and old books. His main hobby was bird watching, which took him all over the world when time allowed. Even in the rain forest he managed to look too tidy, clothes just that little bit too expensive.

Staring out of the train window he wasn't even daydreaming really, just looking out of the window at the scenery rushing by and letting his thoughts bob around. Last weekend's fiasco with Helen, where to go for a vacation, how to hold down or divert that young fellow from Princeton who was so pushy for more responsibility.

Summer was coming fast, and the grasses and rushes alongside the Delaware River (and, further along, the New Jersey Meadowlands) were growing taller and green. As they passed a deserted warehouse near Newark, two boys, scruffy, twelve or fourteen years old, watched the train go by. They stood on an abandoned loading dock and stared intently at the train, studying it almost. Too old to do something embarrassing like waving to the train, they were, nonetheless, riveted by it.

It must be some game, he thought, something to do with counting the cars. Or perhaps they had put pennies on the line for flattening.

We used to do that, he thought.

In that instant, he was transported back to the days when he and his friend – what was his name, damn. Oh yes, Neil. He and Neil would spend hours hanging around the train tracks in the meadows, meadows like these, at the foot of the town. How many years was it? Well, say he had been 12 or 13, then it was some thirty-plus years ago. Trains were different then. It was the very end of the days of the steam railways in Britain. He tried to remember the terms; they were all different in England. A freight car was a goods van, the passenger car was a carriage. The caboose was the guards' van. The locomotive was the engine and the thing behind it with all the coal was the tender. Soon it all came back: engineer – driver, conductor – guard – track – line, switch – points, semaphore – signal.

The most glamorous of all those old steam locomotives had names and were used only to pull the crack, passenger trains. His favorite was the *Duchess of Atholl*, and he'd even had the Hornby model train set with a oo-gauge *Duchess of Atholl* in the old London, Midland and Scottish Railway colors of maroon and black. It made real smoke and pulled three old-fashioned Pullman coaches in cream and brown. Whatever happened to his old model trains? Oh, he knew alright. When he went to college, his mother gave them away.

He half-opened his eyes to survey the unglamorous Metroliner car, and then let his thoughts stay fixed on those far-off days. Grabbing at every scrap of information recalled.

He and Neil would hang on the five-barred gate that

blocked the farmer's track over the train lines and the trains would go by only a few feet from their heads. Well, perhaps twenty, even forty if they were on the far side, the "down" line. Very occasionally, one of the shorter goods (meaning freight) trains would be held up by the signals just short of the station, which itself was hidden around the curve three miles north. When that happened there was the chance to race down the side of the tracks to where the engine stood hissing and panting. The driver might lean out and shout, "Hello!" They would dream of being invited on board. Which never happened.

Once it had, though. He and the rest of the family had been traveling to some small town to the west. It was so long before he took up train watching that he never knew where it had been: never remembered to ask his father. As they waited on the platform of the tiny country station, the train came in. Three or four coaches of the really old-fashioned sort with no interconnecting corridor (and therefore no toilets), pulled by an ancient 0-6-0 steamer, probably of pre-World War I vintage. It stopped; they got on. The guard waved his green flag and blew his whistle for the driver to know it was clear to leave. Nothing moved; they waited.

Then a filthy face, under a dark blue cap, appeared at the carriage window. The driver.

"It's Mr. Halliday, isn't it?"

"Yes. Good afternoon," replied his father in his best bank-manager manner.

"Good day to you, sir. Our chapel came to see you about a mortgage last year. Thought I recognized you."

Then the incredible moment.

"Would your boy like to ride in the cab, up to the next station? He'd be quite safe."

Philip had looked at his mother, knowing that she was thinking about how dirty he would get.

Another miracle. His father said, "Yes."

And so he did, once, when he was about nine, ride on the footplate of a real steam engine. Going all of 15 miles an hour through the green English countryside on a simply perfect day. And he did get dirty because the fireman swung his long-handled shovel mightily and the open door to the firebox let out a tremendous heat that made him rub his sweaty face with his coal-dusty hands. It was perfect.

His older sister, who never would have been allowed to go up there in her good, pink frock, was not even asked. And never forgave him. Not even years later when they talked about the old days. She was always angry about that day. And to be fair, in this case he agreed; it was a bit mean. Although he doubted he had thought so at the time.

The Metroliner slowed, which meant that he had daydreamed all the way to New York, tunnel and all. Philip pulled himself awake with a bit of a jerk, noting to himself how little he was looking forward to this arrival. If ever there was a monument to the loss of glamour of train travel it was New York's Pennsylvania Station with its mean, low passages and depressing décor. It was the same every time he went to New York. Penn Station put him off. He hated this place and therefore never really appreciated New York as he should. He often wondered what it would be like to arrive every time at Grand Central Station, with its monumental stairs and cathedral-like ceilings. It would be like going to a different city.

CHAPTER 2

It did not turn out to be a good day. He excused himself early from lunch – sensible soups and salads, not like the boozy lunches of the old days when he'd started in this business after Harvard Business School – and walked briskly up a few blocks of Wall Street and back again to try to clear his head. What was wrong with him? He was in such a sour mood. Nothing was as good as it used to be.

"I should never have started thinking about those damned trains." He muttered to himself as he waited for the elevator back to the twentieth floor. But he also knew, he saw as clear as day, that he simply did not enjoy all this anymore.

After the meeting ended, his senior partner drew him aside.

"Interested in what you said back there, Philip. Do you think you would have time to expand that viewpoint a little? Might be something in it."

And then the warning bell sounded.

"Perhaps you should take a little time off to develop your ideas."

No one was ever asked to take time off. If ideas were to be "developed" you did that as you went. This was not a university. Something *else* to worry about.

No dinner was arranged, it being understood that the participants would scatter back to their homes in Westchester, the Upper East Side, Philadelphia, and beyond. Philip had no way of avoiding his colleague from Baltimore, who could talk shop until he dropped of exhaustion. So he was stuck with him in the taxi and on the southbound Metroliner.

A nice enough fellow. Philip pretended to sleep; except that as the train rumbled out of the tunnel and started to cross the New Jersey Meadowlands again, he looked out for the two boys. Of course, they were not there. It was getting dark and they were safe at home. Or he hoped they were.

But he was sad that they weren't there, and he realized that he had deliberately chosen a seat on the left of the train, in the window, so as to look for them. He closed his eyes again.

His colleague pulled out a book and read while Philip lay back in his seat. He had never actually slept on a train; it wasn't even worth trying. His mind drifted back again to the boys watching the trains and then quickly to himself and Neil, by the London Midland and Scottish Railway, whiling the hours away doing nothing except talking, hanging on to the gate, and watching the occasional train. They hadn't been idle. But he couldn't really remember what they had done to pass the time.

He remembered games of soccer – two boys is too few and Neil was always shorter but stronger. They also cycled endlessly round and round the field nearest the tracks where someone, presumably older kids who were there in the evenings, had created a sort of miniature cycle speedway or racetrack.

Surely, in fact, on that side of the railway lines the meadows themselves had actually been some sort of deserted town playing fields. On the other side was farmland. That would explain the remnants of two tennis courts with iron wire fencing and posts but no nets. There had been a hut that they had used as a combination wicket/backstop for games of cricket that summer. He had been better than Neil at cricket, so Neil didn't often want to play. The cricket ball was very hard and unfriendly, but it was sissy to use a tennis ball. Plus, if you hit it properly, any ball went too far, and it was a bore to go get it. Two is too few for cricket as well as for soccer.

Sometimes Neil's younger brother, John, had come with them. Like Neil, John was a bit chubby. He was a mummy's boy and a bit of a nuisance. He hadn't had any interest in train spotting. It had bored him. He was more interested in putting pennies on the track or the even more dangerous game of throwing sticks at the wheels of the trains as they went by.

There had been a girl sometimes, too. A strange, silent

girl, about their age, who would arrive on her bicycle, usually wearing a school uniform, and stand by the gates to watch the trains. She collected the numbers, too. But she never spoke: he had never known her name. Neil had thought she was very pretty. Well, and so had he. Odd, that girl, mysterious and silent but also companionable. Then after a while she had stopped coming.

But now the Metroliner was running through the northern part of Philadelphia. Philip gathered his briefcase, addressed a few words to his colleague in order to be polite and, waiting until they had passed the usual landmark of the Zoo, stood up and made his way to a door.

The rest of his trip home was on a different kind of train - a commuter train of the South East Pennsylvania Transportation Authority. Actually, this one was a set of old Reading Railroad rolling stock dating from the 1930s, but it took him up to Chestnut Hill quite efficiently and by 9:30 he was home. He walked off toward his house grinning at the thought of all this railroad nostalgia, until he remembered again the words of the senior partner. It has been a straightforward warning.

CHAPTER 3

That night, Philip killed him yet again. The man in his dreams; in the dark building, as usual, the same man as before.

At 1:30 am he woke trembling, the musty smell of the strange place still in his nose. An old enemy, this dream. He knew that the only way to shake it off was to lie there and try to recall every detail. If he could ever find out who the man was... what it meant.

But on this night, like all the others, most of the details had faded away before he fully woke. All that was left was this terrible feeling of guilt, uncertainty, and plain fear.

He got up at the usual time – 7:00 am. He showered, shaved and made his usual breakfast. Every day, while the kettle was boiling for tea, he poured a glass of fresh orange juice from the large jug he got each week from the Farmer's Market and carefully measured equal amounts of bran flakes and corn flakes into a bowl with some brown sugar. He always ate by the window in the southeast facing living room of this house without a wife. As he ate, he skimmed through the paper while the radio gave the latest news headlines and weather forecast.

All the while this morning, his stomach churned, and his head throbbed. At 8:27 he caught the commuter train into town and by 9:15 was in his office on Market Street where he usually stayed until 6:30 or 7:00. There was no one at home to rush back to. On the train, for the hundredth time recently, he thought how dearly he would love to have a dog.

But no dog. And no wife. She had walked out eight years before, and he couldn't blame her. He had always been a workaholic, even now when he rather hated it all. She wanted to go to parties, theater, movies, dances. He wanted to work, or if not work, read. The house was still piled high with books. He and Helen had turned out not to be able to have children. Neither of them had wanted to adopt. Perhaps that had been selfish. They were still friends.

He had bumped into her at an unavoidable City Hall reception just a week earlier. They had made a mistake in getting together for lunch over the weekend. For a moment he thought he was going to enjoy it; he wanted to see her again. And perhaps she had felt the same way, but they spent the whole meal talking (or rather he listened while she talked) about her latest successes in her job. She had moved to a new firm specializing in dealing with workers who were laid off, something they were starting to call "out-placement." It was going to be a tremendous growth field, she said, and he privately agreed. Perhaps he would soon need that sort of counseling himself. In the end, he had been glad to get away.

Definitely divorced, their marriage had been a terrible mistake. He had tried to make her into a clone of himself, and when that failed it turned out they had nothing to share. It was easy to feel very guilty about his years with Helen. If she was doing well now, it was despite him; worse, it was probably because he was no longer there.

As he sat on the morning train reading the rest of the paper, he wondered, not for the first time, whether she had been right. He should try to be more outgoing. Here he was, at forty-five: fit, active, a decent tennis player and excellent golfer, well-off and not bad looking in a serious sort of way. But he had no social life at all. No real friends. And where was it all heading? Where would he be at seventy?

Halliday spent the day taking out his worries vis-vis the senior partner on his staff. He harassed them about overdue reports, chivvied them into off-the-cuff assessments of various projects, ordered more reports with tighter deadlines, and covered his desk (and his secretary's) with computer printouts that she could understand far better than he.

Lila, his secretary, was a tall, skinny woman with a

rather too-prominent nose. She had a mind like a razor but insisted on being called a secretary when she was really a senior administrative assistant. It was a kind of upside-down snobbery that he never understood. Every night she disappeared to a large family in North-East Philadelphia and a husband who was a part-time jazz pianist, and a part-time cab driver. She dressed soberly, acted sensibly, and ran the whole office. She was known to everyone as, "Dragon Lady."

Philip asked her to stay late, and she sent out for chicken sandwiches, a ritual when a long evening was in the works. Over coffee and wonderful, dry chicken breast with avocado ("whole wheat, easy on the mayo") they, or rather she, assessed the situation.

"The fact is, Mr. Halliday, this office is performing extremely well. Only one member of staff..." she jerked her head in the direction of the cubicle of the latest hire from Wharton, "...is behind last year. On average we are out-performing the market by one-and-a-half percent. Our average costs per account are well within industry norms."

"Yes," he interrupted her. "But I'm getting the distinct message from you-know-who. What are you not saying?"

"You have always asked me to be frank, Mr. Halliday. So I will be. There are two areas that would be worrying me if I were the New York office. Don't mind me saying this, but your own accounts have not all done as well as, say, the top twenty in New York. Partly that's because you have so much on your plate. But..."

"Keep going."

"The associates are more worried about the future, about the chances of real market growth in the next two years than they will tell you. They are looking to you for a bit more leadership and guidance. Actually, they're a bit scared."

CHAPTER 4

The next morning, the face in Philip's bathroom mirror was even more haggard. He'd hardly slept at all.

He had come to call it the "death dream." Sometimes the details afterward were so obscure that it really wasn't a proper dream. He awoke, however, with an overpowering sense of guilt. Always, there was a death somewhere in the dream. Not even that he had caused it, even, but somehow, he felt responsible. Always there was just the guilt, like a blow to the solar plexus. Sometimes the details were explicit: the faceless man, hitting his head against the wall of that – what? – that *place*.

Now he'd had the death dream two nights in a row. That had never happened before. In fact, he hadn't had the dream at all since Helen had left. Until now.

That same morning, as Philip Jerome Kennedy Halliday lay miserably awake in Philadelphia, it was already seven am in England. On the outskirts of a small market town, a schoolteacher was going through her pre-breakfast routine. She stood more or less in the middle of the bedroom, close enough to see out across the fields but not so close that anyone could see in. She always kept the light off – in the winter she kept the curtains drawn – for fear that somewhere across the fields, in those houses they had just put up on Spinney Road, someone would see her.

Wearing a tracksuit over bra and underwear, she went through the brief routine of stretching exercises, designed to keep her limber and set her up for a long day, that she had found in a women's magazine long ago. That finished, she started to pull on a slip, only to stop to wonder whether it was still cool enough to wear an undershirt (she called it a vest). Watching herself in the large mirror of the dressing table, she rubbed her hand across her stomach. She had kept her figure very well. Of course, it helped that she had always been slim. But these underclothes! Why did she always wear these plain cotton, white underclothes for school? She slipped her hand under the pile in the dresser drawer to the pale green, satin set, cool and smooth. No, those were for Sundays.

Shrugging off the thought, she then took out a white undershirt of fine wool and put it on, plus a half-slip. Next came a medium-weight, rose-colored, wool sweater and a "sensible" skirt of dark tartan design. There was no need to wonder about the choice of "sensible" shoes with low heels and plenty of support. She would be on her feet for most of the next eight hours.

No makeup on a school day, just a touch of lipstick. She looked anxiously in the mirror. At 42 she was, she guessed, still an attractive woman, tall and slim, but lines were coming around her eyes and mouth and her dark, chestnut hair – once her crowning glory, now cut to shoulder length – might just be showing a little gray. Her skin was cool and pale, showing off her hair to advantage. As this was nearly the end of term, she was not really surprised to find that she looked tired and tense. But still, she had to wonder.

Downstairs in the kitchen, breakfast was a mindless routine. And silent. She never bothered with the wireless and the news could wait for the evening paper. Boil the water, set out a bowl of cereal, make the tea. Eat and drink. Rinse the dishes and out the door. On this morning she paused at the garage door. Her little two-bedroom brick house was exactly like every other one on the new street. But behind the houses were still the open fields and then woods, scrubland really, that when she was a child they called "The Pignuts" because of the roots of the pignut – like a big cow parsley – that medieval pigs had once foraged for there.

That line of woods should have been completely timeless. But over to the far side, more houses were coming. The field there ended in a bulldozed mass of red clay. Everything was changing. For a moment she looked over the woods, her arms pulled tight across her chest, although it wasn't very cold on this late May morning. Then she got out the tiny Ford and drove briskly off to school.

At the other end of town stood a cottage that had been built 150 years before the schoolteacher's. A row of cottages side-by-side, two-up-and-two-down. Privies still stood at their backs, across a narrow yard, although the council had, about 20 years ago, insisted on installing indoor drains and plumbing.

The owner, or rather the renter, of number 3 was still in bed and normally would have been for an hour or two more. There was little to rouse for. He had no real job but made a living by salvaging scrap that he loaded into a pathetically battered, old car, kept out at the back. A wily, some said cunning, old man who no one liked. In the pub he would appear at your elbow and cadge a half-pint. He always seemed to be around the market on market days and fed himself half the time on the vegetables that the stall owners threw away at the end of the day. He burned their discarded wooden and cardboard boxes in his fireplace.

This morning, although it was only 7:00 am, he also was wide awake, staring at the sky through the dirty windowpane and thinking about the old days. He hated thinking about things past. It made him angry, and when he was angry, he would drink and that often meant finishing the day in a scuffle somewhere. He was always trying to remember not to get into trouble. He had scars and a limp to remind him. But people were such sods, such bastards! Today was going to be one of the bad days.

He got up quickly, putting on the shabby clothes he had worn for the last month or more. There were no mirrors in the house: even when he shaved, which was rarely, he did it without help from a looking glass, as he called it. He knew too well what he looked like: his crooked nose, dirty, gray hair, scars across the cheek. In a cupboard in the kitchen was a bottle of Courage beer. He drank it and went out across the yard to piss in the outhouse, knowing that it would infuriate his neighbors, the "wogs" – Jamaicans or something – with their miserable children calling names after him when they thought he couldn't hear. Then he set out across the town, on foot, lurching as he did because of his shattered hip and leg, looking for something.

Close to the middle of the town were some rows of paired "semi-detached" houses built in the 1920s when the town was prosperous from farming and the knitting mills that had been set up before World War I. Here a large man was already finishing his breakfast at this, for him, late hour of 7:00 am. Although he seemed huge, he was only six foot one, but he had a big, square head and a ruddy face from being outdoors. Mostly he had an imposing presence that made him seem larger than he actually was. Or he thought it did. But now he was putting on extra weight, was slowing down a little, had given up soccer with the younger men, and spent more time in the pub playing darts.

This man was a policeman, a sergeant in the uniformed branch. Left school at 16, entered the army as soon as possible, and then became a copper: PC Plod. He knew he was not the smartest. It had taken longer than anyone thought possible for him to make sergeant. In the end, he did it mostly on the basis of his enormously detailed knowledge of the town and its people. He walked the town and missed nothing. Old ladies loved his solid and reassuring presence. Shifty types avoided him and thereby made themselves even more obvious. But many ordinary folk also felt uneasy when he was around. He was a bit too sure of himself, too much of a presence. One wondered what things would be like if there was a problem. Was this a man who took shortcuts, trod a little carelessly over people's rights? He seemed almost a caricature from the old days when the bobby on the beat dispensed justice with the back of his hand, or even his fist and truncheon, and nobody knew or dared complain.

He ate breakfast in silence, as did his wife across the table. Their two children were already upstairs getting ready for school, leaving their parents to look at each other over the jam pots, salt and pepper and the vinegar bottle from last night's meal. Neither the policeman nor his wife bothered much with reading a paper. They sat and ate their eggs and toast, no longer angry with each other – that had passed last night – but miserable. Just another row, and each wondering how to patch it up and when.

As soon as he could, he got up, wiped his mouth, and walked out of the back door without saying a word. Then the door opened again; without saying a word he came back in, gave his wife a quick kiss, and then left. She smiled happily to herself and started to clear away the dishes.

CHAPTER 5

The staff found Philip unusually intense that morning. In the end, his talk to them was a bravura performance. They listened to his ideas and eagerly started dissecting how they would handle things, categorizing their clients and their investments in the light of his terribly simple but difficult instructions – the age-old problem was to find the right stocks for long-term stability and growth.

He had impressed them. He was their leader again. He had been right in '87, he was probably right about '88. Lila watched through slightly narrowed eyes, seeing the exhaustion behind the intensity of the discussion. But she simply assumed that he had been up all night making sure that this throw of the dice was the right one.

After the meeting, he sat in his chair and stared at the Philadelphia skyline, thinking about going home for the rest of the day, but unwilling to do so. He didn't particularly want to be at home alone, so he stayed. Lila looked in at 5:30 to say goodbye.

"Great going, boss. Just what they all needed. See you tomorrow, keep the faith."

He smiled and waved, knowing that she really meant, "just what we wanted," not "they." But that was alright. Certainly, it was what he had needed to do for some time. He felt good about all that. But not much else.

He tried a movie and ate out at an Italian restaurant where the food turned out to be too greasy for his stomach, with too much garlic. When he got home, he crunched some Tums and thought about bed.

First, he gave in to the idea of a large scotch. It helped him fall asleep. But he woke at about 1:00 am and then tossed and turned worrying about the office, Helen, his empty life, and the death dream, until 3:00 am when he reached over and turned off the alarm, falling into a deep sleep until after 9:00 am when he called the office and told them he would be late.

He had worked out a long time ago why the ancients had thought the heart was the seat of the emotions. Whenever there was stress, he felt the "heartburn" in his stomach long before his head had isolated the problem. Indigestion, ulcers, and gastric reflux had been his constant companions since college. And now anxiety roamed around the hollow of his rib cage like an animal. His sternum was sore with the empty, gnawing pain. His head, usually the reliable organ, was on strike. He stumbled miserably to the bathroom.

Over the years he had often thought about consulting a doctor about his dreams. Instead, he read a few books. Actually, he browsed them at bookshops, for it turned out that bookshops were full of tomes on amateur and professional psychology. They all said there really wasn't anything to worry about. It was just that he was in over his head – either in his work or his private life (the days with Helen). It was some kind of guilt, but of course, he hadn't killed anyone. The death was perhaps the death of his grandparents, or more probably figurative, signifying that he felt deeply guilty about someone; so it must be Helen. Or he was doing something that could make him a social outcast; so it was the fear of losing his clients' money. Charles Darwin had this problem. He wrote in his diary, when he first articulated the theory of evolution, that "it is like confessing to a murder."

He had been pushing Helen, pushing the people at the office. After the divorce, and after things had settled down at the office, he stopped having the dream. Now the senior partner was pushing him, and it had come back.

When Philip took the train into town, deep in thought, he scarcely noticed the stops and almost went past Suburban Station. On an impulse, he did so anyway and got off at 30th Street, the junction with the mainline Amtrack system. The walk back to "center city" would be good for him.

He walked through the great hall past lines of people waiting for Amtrack trains to the north and south, and even one west – to Pittsburgh and beyond. As he did so, he started to get a tickling little doubt. Apart from the senior partner's threat, could it be that his dream was associated in some way with Cottisthorpe? Had it come back because he had been reminiscing, going back all those years? Those damn trains, Neil Holyroyd, and Cottisthorpe.

As he strode down John Fitzgerald Kennedy Boulevard, his mind started to race. Cottisthorpe: over all these years he had never been back there.... was there a connection? Once he had started thinking about those early days, his dream came back. Suppose his dream really did have something to do with his childhood in that small English town. Perhaps he should go back – visit old places, even find old friends. He needed a break anyway.

It might even be fun to explore old haunts. But he had never wanted to go back there before; had he been avoiding it all these years? Yes, he had to admit he had. Why?

CHAPTER 6

Six weeks later; the middle of July. Philip Jerome Kennedy Halliday walked through the "green" line of customs at London Airport feeling grubby from having sat confined in a British Airways plane for seven hours. Even the bigger-than-average business class seat could not make it a comfortable journey. He needed a shower.

Even so, it was good to be away finally. With the office on a more-or-less even keel. And he desperately needed a complete break. "Take a little time off!"

After an expensive taxi to St Pancras Station ("the hell with the cost, I'm bushed") a fast train, painted an odd yellow color took him north. He noted, as he always did on European trains, that the "modern" styling of plastic and aluminum (aluminium) seemed dated, somehow fixed to the 1960s; functional, but less welcoming than the decor of traditional American trains. But the train ran very fast and silently, swaying from side to side enough to make walking in the aisle difficult.

How many times, he wondered, had he been in England but carefully not taken this journey north? When his parents were alive, he had visited them on the south coast. They had retired early but still died young. Part of the generation that lived through the deprivations of two world wars and a great depression, they were always more care-worn and older-looking than their contemporaries in well-fed America.

After that, he still drove occasionally south to the gardens and warmth of Sussex and Kent, or west to the odd beauty of Devon and Cornwall. Once he had driven northeast, through the flat East Anglian countryside of Suffolk and Norfolk, the old kingdoms claimed from the sea and crisscrossed with dikes and ditches, dotted with lakes and marshes. He remembered having been surprised at the beauty of the Suffolk landscape and its absence of large towns. But never north; he never went to Cottisthorpe.

He was nervous; anxious. He didn't know what to expect of today. What was he getting into, riding this train through the industrial sprawl of Bedfordshire and Northampton, into the East Midlands of Leicestershire, Nottinghamshire and Derbyshire?

After an hour, drab urbanization finally gave way to a few fields. It was actually hot. A cloudy day, threatening rain, that gave the passing landscapes and cityscapes an unrelenting uniform grayness. Even the occasional splash of red or orange on the billboards around Luton and Bedford seemed defeated by the general drabness. And in the process, they induced in Philip a sense of his own dull futility. It was all stupid, this trip, he thought, especially as he stood in the gloom of the Leicester station waiting for a "stopping train."

But when real farmland and hedgerows started to pass the windows of the two-car diesel commuter train, the colors of the landscape started to fit together. Philip sat straighter in his seat and put his head near the window to increase his field of view. He scarcely noticed the stop in Loughborough. Now there were low-rising hills, small rivers lined with willows, and occasional stretches of canal. Crows and magpies, a few rabbits in the hedges along the fields. Small mounds clothed with trees standing out in the middle of grazing land. Sheep, cows, and a few horses.

The colors all matched now, the muted greens and grays, dark yellows and browns, the dull white and silver of the water. Suddenly he sighed; he had come back.

A particular stretch of river caught his eye just long enough for him to wonder whether it was familiar when the trains began to slow down again. Looking at his watch, he saw that this was it. Without his really noticing, they had reached Cottisthorpe.

The train had come in exactly on time, 12:32 pm, and the station seemed exactly as he remembered it. Two sets of tracks with a platform on either side. At the south end, a steep iron footbridge took passengers over to the other side. Just like in any model railway.

Here where he had alighted (one tends to "alight" from a train in England) was the only simple building – a glass-windowed waiting room with old, heavily varnished wooden benches and a tiled floor and the "booking hall" where one bought tickets and where timetables were displayed in iron framed glass cases. New since his time was a small counter selling papers and, of course, candy (sweets) of every possible description. It also sold, as far as he could see without being obvious, an ambitious array of girlie magazines.

Despite himself, he did not open the door to the empty waiting room. It was just the same, smelling of stale tobacco smoke, rather like a billiard parlor but with a faint overlay of urine. And the fireplace was evidently still used, as fresh ashes had been blown out by a down-draft from the chimney.

He turned to find himself face-to-face with some kind of railway official.

"Yes, sir. Can I help you, sir."

This too, was exactly what he remembered. The sort of schoolmaster-ish voice of petty officialdom that had never failed to make him squirm. The words were helpful, the tone said: "Now then, just what are you doing? It's my job to make sure you don't do whatever it is you might be thinking of doing." A challenge, delivered by an elderly man with narrow, sloping shoulders and a sad little mustache who could have been pushing Philip and his 12-year-old friends off the platform thirty years before. He was dressed, as they always were, in what might have been a uniform or might have been an old gray suit with a railway badge on his lapel.

For a moment Philip hesitated, then caught himself. He looked the man over carefully, especially noting the badly scuffed gray, suede shoes turned over at the heel.

"Well, no, I am sure you can't."

The Station Master, for this was not just a porter, seemed not to notice the rebuff, giving Philip a fleeting moment to wonder whether he had imagined it all.

"Taxis are outside, sir."

So he has me perfectly pegged as a foreigner. Well, that's okay. After all, I don't have much of an English accent left, he thought. Philip smiled and the station master smiled weakly back.

Philip left through the "Booking Hall," no more than a high-ceilinged room with a ticket window, where a young woman with two children was bending down to speak at the gap at the bottom of the plate glass window. The children were fussing, dressed too warmly for such a muggy, summer day. One had a runny nose.

Outside the station, the same almost circular forecourt stretched on one side to an old factory and on the other to the bridge that carried the main road over the tracks. There were two taxis out there, both drivers trying not to look too interested in the possibility that Philip was a fare. He waved in their direction and the first one pulled forward, the driver getting out reluctantly to open the trunk (the boot) for Halliday's two suitcases. Philip got in, asking for the White Horse Hotel on Victoria Street.

"Aye, I know where it is."

As the taxi left the station parking lot and started to draw into the traffic on the main road, Philip leaned forward.

"Wait. Could we go out along the road here, back towards the river?" Stupid question.

"We'll go anywhere you like, guv. Just tell me. American you are, I'd guess. Is this your first time in Cottisthorpe?"

"No, I actually used to live here once. Look, go right here and then follow along, there used to be a place where the river crossed under the road and there was an old mill. I can't remember the name."

"Aye, that's Oakley's Mill. Lovely meals they do there. Will you be planning to stop for lunch?"

"Meals?"

"Oh aye, been turned into a nice restaurant, lovely it is, so I'm told. A bit pricey for me, I expect."

"Oh, well, I just want to see."

"Not much to see, if you ask me, but the meter's running and you're the boss. I've got all day. Take you to Skegness if you want."

Once over the railway, the road weaved along between high hedges. A two-foot-high verge of grass marked how the road had sunk over the years. Philip could only see the fields beyond through the bases of the hawthorn hedge, noting that there was a great deal of litter around, mostly plastic bags that he recognized as being from potato chips (crisps, here).

The car was starting to go fast, but Philip wanted to see the countryside.

"No, slow down."

Now the driver was sullen, shrugging his shoulders and slowing down to about 25 mph. Philip felt stupid. He could rent a car tomorrow and do all this himself.

The road swung away from the town and almost immediately the hedges looked greener and fuller. The sun came out briefly and lit up oaks, willows and low stands of elder and hazel. In the far distance was the railway line, raised on a low embankment, and between them, the silver of the river showed now and then between the trees. He watched eagerly, forgetting the driver, as the river came closer, and then, all too soon, they were pulling into a giant parking lot.

"Here you are, squire: Oakley's Mill."

Philip was disappointed. It wasn't at all what he remembered. He had actually missed the river running beneath the road, perhaps because the water here was no more than six feet across and the bridge only a slight rise in the road.

The old mill buildings of faded red brick had been painted bright white. The gravel parking lot was full of expensive-looking cars. The mill itself was bigger than he remembered, a three-story building, high rather than broad, built next to the mill race with two lower buildings by its sides. Across the way was the old farmhouse, now also painted white, with red geraniums in tubs.

"What's your pleasure, mate."

Lack of sleep was hitting him hard. "Oh, let's just go to the hotel."

Now the driver turned up the speed again and Philip didn't argue. They shot back along the road as he examined the view from the other side of the road.

In the far distance, the fields rose up gently to some low hills, sparsely dotted with older trees, again mostly oaks. It was more like a park than farmland. It was on those hills, surely, that he and Neil Holyroyd had gathered mushrooms on cool summer mornings. And Neil's mother cooked them in butter in a skillet so that they tasted wonderful – once Philip finally plucked up his courage to try one. Ever after, he was disappointed with his own mother who never wanted to try anything like that. Philip's mother, from the London suburbs, had a very parochial view of gastronomy. Garlic, indeed, most herbs and especially things like fried onions, were for her examples of why European countries gave in to the Nazis. "Nasty things," she had said when he brought her some cool, white mushrooms. Very different from Neil's mother, who would always laugh at such hesitations. "Don't you trust me, luvvie? I know all about mushrooms, I'm a country girl."

Soon the taxi was climbing the bridge back over the train tracks. The driver slowed as they entered a narrow street that wound uphill towards the town center, first crossing over a classic hump-backed canal bridge. This at least, was familiar. But then he saw that a whole part of the town had been knocked down, new buildings and even new streets had been put in. Blocks of flats and shops stood where once, if his memory was right, there had been terraced houses and an old Wesleyan chapel.

"This is all new."

"Hardly, mate. This was here before my time."

Philip noticed for the first time that the driver was probably only in his mid-twenties.

However new, this part of the town was already shabby. As the taxi made its way through the new parts and then into more remembered ground again, Philip found that he was looking at the people on the street to see if he recognized any of them. Many looked vaguely familiar because the whole town seemed not to have changed very much. But there was no one he knew. Days later, he realized that when he scanned faces for someone he might know, he fixed on people in their 20s and 30s. But the 20 and 30-year-olds of today would be the children of his old acquaintances or school friends.

One other thing was very different. Many of the people on the street were Asian, the men wearing turbans and the women saris. Included were a few Black people, presumably from the West Indies. All wore bright clothes contrasting with the English drab grays and brown – bright, exotic, almost-reds, orange, vivid greens. They moved differently from the English -- more easily and confidently, less bowed down by the cares of the world. They were mostly younger. The English people on the streets were either older (his age or more) or young people with small children.

Philip Jerome Kennedy Halliday took all this in as the taxi traversed less than half a mile before making two unfamiliar turns and dropping him right at the front door of the White Horse Inn.

In his day this had been mostly a pub, with simple rooms (for single, male, "commercial travelers"). But the AA book said it was now a pleasant hotel, recommended for tourists visiting the nearby attractions of Charnwood and Nottingham Forests with their legends of Robin Hood and Sir Walter Scott's *Ivanhoe*. Standing in the small, paneled lobby he saw partly open doors to the right, with gleaming brass and frosted glass, leading into a traditional bar, replicated in a thousand pubs across the country. A door facing to the left was identical except for this legend "dining room." Next to the reception desk a set of stairs, carpeted in a hideous floral design, evidently led up to the rooms.

A wonderfully jolly woman appeared as if by magic from behind the desk. She must have weighed well over 200 pounds, but her flowered dress had been made for someone a little smaller. She had masses of oddly yellow curls and a bit too much red lipstick. But instead of looking silly, she looked like every childrens book image of the farmer's wife, flushed from a morning baking. Indeed, there was now a wonderful smell of hot cakes and sugar.

"Oh, have you been waiting long? I've been that busy this morning, what with that bus load of folks leaving and it being my day to bake for the social." She paused, "For the old folks, at church this afternoon," as if Philip should have remembered that.

"You'll be Mr. Halliday. Everyone calls me Queenie. Feast or famine here. Last night 20, today just you. Shall you just go on up and get settled and we'll do all the paperwork later? That'd be best."

Without pausing for breath, she bustled around to pick up a bag, as Philip protested.

"No, here. We'll just shove 'em in the lift."

He had missed a tiny elevator in the corner. There was just room for the two bags. Mrs. Henslow, for evidently this must be the manager, shut the door and gently pushed him toward the stairs.

"No point in carrying them. We'll take the stairs and call 'em up after us."

Which they did, and Mrs. Henslow showed him into a small but pleasant room overlooking the back of the hotel. The bathroom was also small, but perfectly adequate with a modern on-piece, fiberglass shower stall (made in Sweden, he later noted). Philip might have found it all a bit spare, except for Mrs. Henslow's energy, expressed in non-stop talking to which he was only half listening. He was searching his memory for whom Mrs. Henslow reminded him. It was not until she had finally left, after showing him towels (never a washcloth in English hotels) and apologizing for the absence of in-room phones, that he worked out that it must be Ma Larkin from *Darling Buds of May*. Except there was something rather more substantial about Queenie. She looked like the type who not only cooked for the socials but also threw out the drunks on Saturday nights.

His room looked out over out-buildings that had once housed horses and their drivers and grooms but were now the kitchens. Beyond were the dark slate roofs of the rest of the town, with the Town Hall rising up like a church in the middle. But he could not see the hills beyond.

He had now been traveling for 20 hours straight. Disgruntled and depressed, and feeling distinctly lonely, he showered and then lay down on the bed and stared at the ceiling. It was warm in the room, and he had expected England to be cold. After a few seconds he sat up against the pillows and looked across the room at the window and the sky beyond. Large clouds had gathered, slow and full of rain. Wishing that he had never come, he thought briefly of home, of the even greater summer heat in Philadelphia. A few large drops of rain hit the window, and then more.

CHAPTER 7

When he awoke, it was dusk: a car door slamming in the yard below the window and disagreeably cheery people calling to each other in almost incomprehensible East Midlands voices.

"Ay up, Jack."

"Andy, you old bugger, how's tha' sen."

These long-forgotten cadences instantly jarred an image. There were men meeting after work, from office jobs and from selling cars and screwdrivers, television sets and children's toys. But they spoke with the tongue and self-confidence of the farmer. Beefy-faced people who knew where they stood and would not budget for anything. Cocky, aggressive when drunk.

He started automatically to translate these regional signatures:

"Ay-up" or "Hey-oop," both greetings meaning "hello," perhaps from "heads-up." And "oo-ya" from "oh, you," an exclamation of surprise. Yes, there below the window:

"OO-ya bugger, ah thowt ah'd backed 'er in just reet." Evidently, someone had parked his car too close to another.

"Bugger" had no more connotation "twerp," in this context. "Sen" meant "self" as in "tha'sen," "hissen," and "yer sen."

Philip felt a familiar shiver of discomfort at these Midlanders of his youth who stood four-square for what they knew and scorned everything different, especially from the South or, worse, abroad. They might take their wives to Majorca or the Algarve for a week's holiday nowadays, but they would gather in groups for their beer and French fries (chips) at cafes only too willing to cater to the English abroad. Once again, he wished he had not come.

An empty stomach, however, drove him downstairs to find the small restaurant beyond the door marked "dining room." All the diners were, like him, alone. Salesmen, he assumed, traveling. He was late.

The menu was simple. No "foreign muck" here. Oxtail soup (bound to be canned, or rather "tinned"), fruit cocktail (ditto) and for the entrees, cold lamb salad, grilled ham and pineapple, or fish of the day – cod cakes, "very tasty" the waiter announced. He wondered briefly what a cold lamb salad would be like but opted for the ham. While he waited, he sipped a scotch and soda (forgetting to simply ask for "whiskey") and looked around.

The waiter, a boy of perhaps no more than 17, now

stood by the door to the kitchen. He wore black jeans, almost dark gray, and a well-pressed white shirt of vaguely Italian or Mediterranean cut, and watched over the room as if each diner were a sacred charge. It took a long time but at last there was a low call and the boy disappeared into the kitchen, returning almost as quickly with a very hot plate on which lay a huge slice of ham, two rings of canned pineapple, several slices of beetroot already staining the ham, and a pile of fluffy mashed potatoes.

Not a woman's dish, thought Philip, piling in with surprising appetite and finding it all very good indeed. In fact, it was all delicious. No microwave here, either.

Having finished at top speed a large portion of the ham and mashed potatoes, Philip waited to see what would happen next. Soon the boy waiter – "'ave yer done, then?" – whisked away the plate and offered the "sweet tray."

Dessert turned out to be a choice among Black Forest cake, canned fruit salad or crème caramel.

"A sweet, sir?"

Resisting the urge to try the crème caramel, Philip asked for coffee.

"Oh, and do you have decaffeinated?"

"Of course, would you like ordinary or cappuccino?"

The cappuccino turned out to be very good. After a second cup, he had revised his opinions. Some things *had* changed.

As he leaned back in his chair, his mind wandered back yet again to the 1950's. There had been almost nowhere to eat in this small, country town. The farmers who brought cows, sheep and pigs to the Thursday cattle market just by the town center had to eat their lunch in pubs – cheese, hard bread rolls and pickled onions, together with pint glasses of warm beer (the cheaper "mild," not the best bitter). A mobile van sold morning tea and hotdogs. This hotel had served lunch to an upscale "county" crowd and dinner to the few traveling salesmen. Almost every businessman or the (few) women, went home for lunch.

There had been a tearoom somewhere, serving morning teas and coffee, a few luncheon sandwiches and afternoon teas (closing: 4:45 pm). And that was all. For a while, young people could buy coffee or a milkshake if they went to the Palace Cinema. Apart from that, there were just the pubs, and in the evenings they served only drinks, and soft drinks on sufferance.

Then in 1959, just as some of his friends were getting their driver's licenses and a bewildering freedom, a small evening coffee bar opened. La Madrid, with a Spanish theme, served espresso coffee from Italy, made in a noisy, hissing machine and served in brown glass cups. Loud folk music played, plus Cliff Richard, Elvis Presley and the Everley Brothers. It was a different world: London, Europe, New York even, who knew? Suddenly girls appeared in town, real girls in attractive clothes (long skirts, real stockings) – amazingly they turned out mostly to be the same girls from the high school, but no longer dressed in those hideous uniforms.

A whole new world of young people, talking, singing,

smoking of course; emerging into a world of their very own, not created by grown-ups (or at least not by their parents or school). The town elders sniffed their disapproval, but to no avail. After just a few months, a town that had not changed since the 1920s, certainly not since the end of the war, entered a modern age. Of course, when he went off to university, he found that every other town in England had discovered espresso coffee long before.

Come to think of it, the "Madrid" had been exactly opposite the entrance to the Cattle Market. Opposite in every way from the shouting, red-faced men in long boots, sacking aprons and flat caps. The lowing, grunting cattle being prodded this way and that; the auctioneer, young and cheekily assured, the smell of manure, the ever-present cold and damp. Nothing so cold as wet, cow-shit-covered cobblestones in February. A fog of breath around each face, humans and cattle alike.

Inside the "Madrid" all was modern, warm, rich, enveloping and ever-so-slightly risqué, it was here that Alan what-was-his-name? From the lower sixth form (grade 12) met the secretary visiting from Nottingham and weeks later she was pregnant. And most of them had never as much as glimpsed a naked shoulder (except for those of sisters of course). While they all merely spent their nights hopelessly wondering about breasts and thighs, Alan had gone for the gold. Philip almost laughed out loud – she hadn't really been pregnant after all, but by the time their friends learned about the wedding, rushed and furtive, she and Aland were firmly ensconced running his father's electrical shop. Perhaps they were still here.

He must have laughed out loud, after all. The only other remaining diner looked over at him sharply – in England you were quiet in restaurants (except in London). The waiter appeared with the bill to sign.

Unembarrassed and still smiling, Philip made his way out. He felt better, almost cheerful, looking forward to exploring the next day. Was the cattle market still there? Surely "La Madrid" would be long gone.

Voices from the bar made him hesitate at the stairs. A happy sound, a woman laughing softly. The harshness of the earlier men calling in the rear yard was gone. He stood for a moment in the empty hall and then pushed open the double, frosted glass doors.

CHAPTER 8

The saloon bar was a large square room full of small tables. The bar itself was huge, gleaming with brass and bottles. A broad-faced, broad-bodied balding man, tall, perhaps 250 pounds, stood behind chatting quietly to an older man sitting at a stool. No one looked up when he entered, or if they did it was quietly and uninterestedly. These were townspeople in their own pub but used to visitors from the hotel.

The room was warm and smokey – people seemed to smoke a great deal more than in the US. Unsure what the protocol would be if he sat at a table – was he supposed to get his drink at the bar first? – he took a stool at the bar, a short way down from the barman.

After waiting just long enough to make the point that Philip was a stranger, the bartender moved down to take his order. Evidently, body language was important here and he had failed the test by taking a stool just a bit too far away. Too close to the older man would have been crowding him; this far looked "stand-offish." The bartender allowed it to appear as though the journey down to Philip was an unnecessary inconvenience.

His face was neither friendly nor unfriendly and therefore, in its careful indifference, hostile. It said "outsider," while it spoke the time-honored phrase:

"What will you have, sir?"

The timing of the hesitation before the "sir" was just a nanosecond too long to be polite.

Philip knew he didn't want the bitter beer – too much of an acquired taste, long lost – and so asked for a whiskey and soda. However, he also knew that whiskey was potentially an "uppish" drink in a public bar. (But at least he had remembered, just in time, that "Scotch" was "whiskey" here.)

Damn, why did he have to feel so sensitive?

With the whiskey and old-fashioned soda siphon was brought an ice bucket with a few absurd chips of ice floating in an inch of water. The meaning was unmistakable: "I know you're a Yank and will want to spoil your drink with ice."

That was easy, he pushed the ice bucket away, trying to look as though he hadn't quite noticed the barman's faux pas in proffering it and moved to a table from the uncomfortable stool. Only three other tables were occupied. At one, a roly-poly man in a red sweater sat with his wife – short and rather pretty in a pink cardigan and tweed skirt – with two younger men, tall and also in sweaters. The three men all had a fit outdoors look, even the chubby, middle-aged one. He wondered if they were farmers until he noticed their odd clothes. Under their sweaters, they had blue dress shirts, and their trousers were black, like their shoes. As he took another sip of the Bell's, it was obvious. They were policeman. Of course, the police station was only just around the corner, or at least it used to be!

At another table was an older couple, in their seventies he guessed, poorly dressed and evidently, making their pint glasses of beer last as long as possible. They sat not talking, just watching the room and clearly had been observing him because, as he looked over, they quickly put their eyes down. Both had pinched faces as if with permanent head colds.

Over against the far wall two couples, early thirties, moderately prosperous looking, sat talking and laughing quietly. The men had beer and the women wine. Presently, one of the men got up and took the empty wine glasses to the bar.

"Two more red, Fred, please."

As he returned to his table, he looked squarely at Philip in polite interest. Philip nodded, which seemed at least not the wrong thing to do.

Philip finished off the whiskey and, as sleep seemed suddenly to be catching up with him fast, headed for the door. The barman called out "good night" (it sounded more like "gu'neet") to which he responded with a nod and shy smile.

Philip lay between the cool, hard sheets wondering just

what terrible dreams he would have now that he was finally here. He got up and looked out over the yard below the window and the black rooftops, shiny with rain. The only light came from the kitchen and the harsher glow of distant streetlamps – the nasty gray-blue, night-time color of towns everywhere. The town hall clock tower was dark and seemed much closer. It was 9:00 pm and the town was totally quiet and asleep.

Deciding he wouldn't sleep after all, he put on the TV out of curiosity. There were the usual four channels, all showing American sitcoms. At 9:20 the BBC started a news program – he was astonished that they still stuck to such irregular scheduling. By the time the weather forecast came on – actually only a report of the weather of the day now past – he was fast asleep. Something woke him up an hour later. He got up to turn it off and then, as he watched the swirling after-glow on the screen recede to a point, slept again.

CHAPTER 9

A sharp knocking on the door woke him. Through the curtained windows it was clearly morning. He groped for the light and as he did so the door opened.

"Morning tea, sir. Did you sleep well?"

Mrs. Henslow, absurdly dressed in leggings, a tight sweater, and a tiny white apron, bustled in like a nurse pulling aside the curtains and letting in bright sunshine. (God, he'd forgotten the ritual of serving morning tea in bed!) She turned off the light without being asked.

"It's a lovely day again, you *are* lucky. Such wonderful weather we are having. Been that hot for days on end, it has."

She picked up the tray from where she had parked it on the dresser top and approached the bed. Obviously, she was going to put it on his lap – just as his mother had when he needed a tray because of being sick in bed with measles or chicken pox. He sat up quickly and as she bent over with the tray, their heads bumped.

Queenie laughed easily, "Whoopsy-daisy. That won't do, will it?"

She had a more southern accent, not local, and smiled happily from that round face and halo of curls.

"Breakfast's downstairs anytime til 8:45. Are you staying long?"

"Three or four days, maybe more."

"That's nice then. In business, are you?"

Obviously, he was the only customer for morning tea, and she could easily stay.

"Just visiting and looking around actually."

"Not much to see here, is there?"

(Oh well, he might as well start now.) "Well, I used to live here years ago, so I'm visiting old places."

"That's really nice – and old friends, no doubt. But don't let me keep banging on. Your tea will get cold, won't it?" And she left.

The tea was strong and, even with sugar, slightly bitter – a not unpleasant memory of childhood.

After breakfast in the empty dining room – resisting "Yorkshire bacon" and "farm-fresh" eggs, he had stuck to cold cereal – he was at a loss as to what he would actually do now that he was here. The first thing seemed to be to stroll around and get his bearings, although there were some places he wasn't even sure he wanted to explore, not just yet anyway. And he might find a familiar face or name.

It was warm but he took a light jacket and was interested to see that the few people on the street at 9:30 were dressed for cold weather, men in thick jackets and women in coats.

After an hour, he discovered that the town had changed most on the north side, around the church. Much of the town center was exactly the same except that all the shops were different, and all of the facades had been modernized. The Palace was now a bingo hall.

The town hall still had the police station and court in the back but the town offices themselves were somewhere else. The old hospital seemed to be closed down, the only activity being a sort of clinic for young mothers and emergencies.

The empty town center, where an open-air market had once been conducted every Thursday and Saturday in the old days, was now a car park, already filling with cars. To the right should lead to a small street with the library and cattle market and yes, "La Madrid." Beyond that should be the town park – "keep off the grass" – and very formal flower beds set out with annuals, all surrounding an old-fashioned bandstand.

None of this seemed to have remained. The cattle market was now a supermarket. The rows of houses, one of which had been converted to the "Madrid," were a parking garage, linked to the supermarket by a bridge over the narrow street. No library, no park. Just buildings vaguely looking like flats and offices. He stopped and immediately someone behind bumped into him.

"Oo-ya, watch out mister!"

"Sorry."

The woman, heading for the supermarket judging by the large, empty shopping bag, half-turned and looked back.

"Are you lost, luv?"

"I thought the library would be somewhere along here."

She laughed. "You're in the wrong street. This is Green Street. Cattle Market Street is the next one up." She waved vaguely towards the supermarket. "Just walk through the shop here, you'll be right."

So he did, discovering that the store was actually several stores in one, already quite full of shoppers, mostly women. He bought a cup of coffee from a counter and walked through to the far exit.

On the other side, he was in no more familiar territory. If this was Cattle Market Street, the market itself was now a block of town offices and he was standing almost exactly where the espresso machine of the "Madrid" had been.

But up to the right he could see the park entrance. He walked up and there, opposite, was the familiar old public library, founded with a gift from Andrew Carnegie whose name was chiseled into the brick above the door. A small, modern addition went off behind, but it was very much the same place. He thought about going in but decided instead to keep walking.

The park was empty and therefore inviting. He wandered around the beds of dahlias, geraniums and nasturtiums. Too garish for his taste but beautifully maintained.

As he sat on a bench to finish the last of his take-out ("take-away," the woman had said) coffee, the sun came out again, lighting up the soft reds of the old houses around the park and giving a gentler color to the gray concrete and stone of the newer buildings closer to town. A chaffinch dropped down by his foot looking for crumbs.

A large policeman in uniform entered at the far end of the park. Philip eyed him casually and was at once aware that, although a good 70 yards away, the policeman was watching him. Philip looked away and then, when the figure in dark blue came nearer, looked again. It was the roly-poly man from the bar last night, now huge under his bobby's helmet – a feature that Philip knew most towns had long since given up in favor of the peaked cap. A sergeant, judging from his stripes; strolling along, several flower beds away, he exuded an air of calm, of being in control. He moved as if ready to pounce, in a graceful stride like the ease with which many large people dance. Philip, feeling somewhat as though he had been made to feel as if he had invaded someone else's turf, got up and walked after him, back towards the library and then to the town center.

He stopped at a small newsagent near the corner of Cattle Market Street and bought the local weekly paper, *The Cottisthorpe Reporter*, and went back to the hotel.

The paper had several items he needed – firms with "cars to hire," the name of a camera shop, and lists of upcoming events. He also scanned the pages carefully for names he might recognize, just as all that morning he had scanned the faces of people on the streets (and found them all strangers). He was looking for names like Onions, Smedly, Ashe, Peabody, Stamper, Berresford, Lakin, Sharples, Parkin, Yeomans, Tunnicliff, Simpkin, Towles – remnants of the various bands of colonists who had swept over the land, mostly from the east, a thousand years ago. None, it seemed, were left.

There was no phone in his room and when he went to the lobby, the receptionist "Doreen" (clearly a relative of Mrs. Henslow) insisted on ordering the "hire car" for him, so he slipped out again to find a sandwich for lunch. Just as well, here in Cottisthorpe they still practiced the odd custom of "half-day closing." All the shops closed at 1:00 pm on Wednesdays.

CHAPTER 10

"I've got your car. Around the corner in Stacey Street; the Ford Garage."

He did not answer.

"Er, sorry, did you hear me? Stacey Street, it's..."

"Oh. I'm sorry. Yes, Doreen. I know where it is. Thank you, I'll find it."

He had been rude, without meaning to be. But yes. Yes, he knew Stacey Street. He had been putting this off, but now he stepped out of the hotel front door and his feet took him automatically first onto the block north and then left into Stacey Street.

Stacey Street had been *his street*. A quiet, double row of genteel stone and brick houses built in the nineteenth century on the foundations of houses that had been there 200 years before. Some had been converted to shops with the owners "living over." They were gracious houses, rather admired by the rest of the town. Narrow alleys between them led to large stable yards at the back where a service road gave access to the garages that had long since been added. Back there, too, kitchens that had been built onto the houses, with bathrooms overhead, all in the local stone.

Number 18 had been a complete house, no shop underneath, and had been his home for three years while his father was the manager of the local bank – Barclay's was the only one back then. Next door had been the optician's shop of Mr. Ainthorp, who had sold him his first pair of binoculars – the World War I field glasses that started him off as a bird watcher.

In his memory, number 18 had been old and cozy, with flagstone floors in the hall and a big fireplace in the living room. There had been fireplaces in the bedrooms too, and when he or his sister had been sick, fires were built there to keep them warm, fires that flickered in the dark in the evenings so beautifully that it was always worth being sick, just for the romance of it all.

In fact, though, the house was often cold, and damp and it drove his mother crazy. Shoes mildewed in the winter damp. Furniture lost its veneer or simply cracked. Car and lorry exhaust fumes seeped in from the street, even through closed windows. But he had been a romantic then and the old stone house, with its eighteenth-century coal cellar and narrow stairs, was a special, magic world. He had a bedroom in the attic and from the small, gabled window could see to the north, all the way to the big hills that framed the town from that side and the dark green of Charnwood Forest.

His parents, particularly his mother, really had hated that house. A large iron stove in the kitchen had to be kept alight all year because it provided not only the means of cooking but also the hot water for the whole house. The whole house was too narrow and inconvenient; too many stairs, too many corners; uneven floors always catching your feet.

But it wasn't there. As he stood on the corner, checking up at the sign to be sure he was in the right place, his heart sank. Stacey Street had been leveled, and in the place of its higgledy-piggledy mixture of styles and colors, sat two rows of red brick, "modern" buildings, four or five stories high on one side, lower on the other. To the left, they ran in an unbroken wall to the far corner. To the right, the higher side, they were in two groups and the nearer one had a large garage in its base. That was where he was heading, obviously. But not happily.

All his adult life he had looked back to the three short years in that house as the beginning of his being aware. It was the anchor of his memory. He had often wondered whether he would have dared to go back to see it. He never had before. Now it was all too late. Another reason why he never should have come.

"What happened? Why did they tear down the old street?"

The youngish woman at the hire desk looked surprised.

"Did you not know about the fire? Yes, the old timber merchant's that used to be in the Bread Street, right behind here, caught fire one night, let's see...perhaps 15 years ago. It spread like wildfire and set light to this side. People were fighting to get out of their houses... It was terrible. There was this awful wind, too, and the fire spread right over the other side, but not past the car park of the Labour Exchange. The fire brigade stopped it there. But all this side and that. Worst fire in Cottisthorpe history. Three folk died even. Did you not read about it?"

"They were lovely houses."

"Did you think? I remember the shops, a bit run down they were. My dad said it was good to clear 'em out and start over. Them old flats was never very nice either, no proper plumbing, and no central heating. The new flats are lovely, I live down on the other side. Ever so convenient for work and for shopping. No use in saving them old places."

"No, I suppose not. Oh well, what about that car."

It was unreasonable, he knew, to expect people to live in a sort of museum. They wanted central heating and "all mod-con." Stacey Street just represented the old and unwanted.

While he had hesitated about visiting Stacey Street, he had already decided there was no need to visit the place they had moved to next – a modern "bungalow" in a new development up the hill. His mother had loved that one;

had cried when they left. But the rooms were small and the ceilings low. Even though his mother loved her kitchen and his father had made a nice garden from the old field in the back, it had no character. And it was too far from his old friends.

Those friends, in fact, assumed that he had taken on airs and was now too good for them. He rarely saw Neil after that, whose family lived in a terraced cottage by the church. They were now in different forms at school. In any case, his new friends were more interesting, and their fathers had money for cars (which his did not, taking his bicycle down to the bank every morning, rain or shine).

Back to the present, Philip! The point of renting the car was to explore, starting with the old meadows and the place where they train-spotted. Somewhere there, on the edge of the water meadows, should be the playing fields and, next to the railway lines, the place where he remembered watching the trains. It was those trains that had brought him back. Everything started from there. That would be his first...what? First test, maybe.

He could see it all in his mind. They would cycle from Neil's house down towards the station and then over to the right. There was a road that ended up as a lane and it led directly to the railway.

The trouble was, the real town no longer fit that memory. He drove rather shakily down towards the station, getting used to the wrong side of the road, but then came to the canal bridge. The canal? Where did that fit in? He didn't remember much about the route of the canal through the town. But surely he had to have gone over it to get to the railway. After a frustrating half-hour, he headed back to the Stacey Street garage and asked for the map he had been too proud to take at the outset.

The map was a minimal photocopied sheet, but he could see approximately where to go. The town had grown like an amoeba, even in this northern end where, in the old days, no one much had wanted to live. The rows of back-to-back terraced cottages had been the closest thing to a slum in Cottisthorpe. Some of those were still standing, but otherwise, there were only neat council-built terraces of three or four, mostly occupied by recent immigrants.

He found his bearings by a small boarded-up factory building, part of the old Minton complex and possibly where Neil's father had worked, and then traced his way back over the canal. Here now, surely, was the long street that had once been the farmer's lane leading to the water meadows. It even began to look familiar.

Some of the remaining cottages had been spruced up here, with odd colors of paints – vivid blues and greens, red and even a purple or two. Beyond this was a group of newer houses in yellow-gray brick – lavatory brick, he and his sister had always called it because public toilets seemed always to be built in that color. Everything was quite clean although there were a lot of apparently broken-down cars. Indian (Pakistani?) women with babies stood at doorways as he drove slowly along, watching him with rather questioning eyes. Well, he didn't blame them; he *was* an interloper.

The road turned a little and then ended in a dead-end with a small circle to turn around. He parked the car at the last house and got out to see if there was a way through on foot. This was definitely the right road (street, he supposed) but it ended here in a high fence, with no apparent passage beyond. Thwarted, he tried the next street over.

This one also ended in a fence, but children had forced an opening off to one side where the fence abutted a large old tree. On the other side, he found the railway lines were surprisingly close – only 30 yards or so away. These new houses had been built right down onto the meadows. A narrow slip of field was all that was left between the backs of the houses and the tracks. To the left, the fence climbed to a low hill that he didn't recognize until he realized that, of course, it was the old refuse tip, now sunken and grassed over. Two scruffy horses, one gray and one dark, almost black, grazed but otherwise, it was empty of life.

He saw that there were no longer any gates to take the lane across the lines. Indeed, there was no lane. The field was no longer connected to the farm over the tracks. In place of the old hedge, a strong wire fence kept the horses and wandering children off the tracks. Nothing remained of the old tennis courts, which in fact must have been behind him where someone's garden now was.

A fiasco: the trip was a terrible fiasco. Everywhere he

looked things had changed. Stacey Street torn down; the meadows built over. Disappointment washed over him as he drove back toward the town center. But the sun was shining nicely again, so he decided on one last venture, retracing the route the taxi driver had taken to Oakley's Mill.

CHAPTER 11

The mill's parking lot was empty (not surprisingly; it was 3:30 pm). He left the car near the road and started to explore on foot. The river here ran fast through a narrow channel out of what had once been the mill race. Just before the bridge, it made a broad turn. On the inner side of the curve, nearest the mill, it almost made a small beach of sand. On the opposite side, a row of willows was dangerously undercut, and one was sagging over the stream. He stepped on the sand for a moment and watched the water ripple by. This at least was just the same: timeless. Then he tried to find a path upstream.

In the old days, this had been a public right of way, much used by fishermen. He was looking for the path, but couldn't find one, even by pushing his way through waist-high weeds almost up to the Mill itself. So he walked around the mill buildings and started upstream again on the other side.

Here there was a definite path, and he could already hear the sound of the weir upstream. Now everything was more familiar. This whole area was part of what had once been a broad swath of water meadow on the north-eastern side of town. The river meandered its way through the lush green in the summer and in the late winter/early spring rains the whole area was flooded, in some points to a couple of feet deep. Silt washing over onto the meadows renewed them and provided rich grazing for the summer and fall.

Early on, someone had worked out that the river and canal could be combined, providing a header pressure for the locks that were needed east and south of town where the canal dropped onto the flatland of Leicestershire and beyond. So, as the canal skirted the side of town, it was for a while both canal and river combined. Just here, above the mill, the river and canal separated again. Essentially a weir had been created –a long stone slash cut into the side of the canal where the river ran back into its old bed and, incidentally, turned the mill, before crossing over the meadows to run at the foot of the mushroom-hunting hills on the other side.

Today was becoming warmer and warmer, and more quiet, the further he walked from the mill. He was conscious only of the whirring of insects and the swishing of the breeze through the willows. A yellow hammer sang and for the first time, he reached for his binoculars. He quickly found the yellow hammer and then other familiar birds like the hedge sparrow, black-capped warbler, chiffchaff, greenfinch, and a willow warbler. There was a marsh tit as well as the inevitable blue tits and great tits. A coot called, presumably from the canal.

One more willow tree and there was the weir, together with a footbridge over to the other side of the canal/river. That was definitely new. Evidently, there was now a path that led down here directly from the town. This was a place to sit and think. In his youth, he had fished here occasionally, and then later it became a haunt for bird watching. This was where he had seen his first kingfisher, and in this journey back through time it would be nice to see another.

Time passed, but no kingfishers came. Some crows argued in the distance and there were far more magpies than seemed right. In addition to the familiar wood pigeon, there were many collared doves, a European immigrant. On the railway embankment beyond the canal a short train went by – but surprisingly quietly – its gently purring diesel a far cry from a pounding, snorting steam train.

This silly little train, like something out of a children's story, seemed to capture all the changes between the Cottisthorpe of his youth and now. It was telling him to go home, there was nothing he could discover here that would help him with the stupid dreams. Coming had been a waste of time; just some kind of useless sentimentality. Everything had changed. He felt terribly sad and lonely, sitting by the tiny river, no more than a stream. And totally out of place. He should just go home.

Now clouds had come over the sun, dark purple and gray, and the breeze had turned to almost a wind. He hurried back along the path ahead of the rain between stands of Queen Anne's Lace, forgetting (as he always had) to watch for nettles. The trees roared in the wind and a few leaves were whisked away ahead of him.

He retrieved his car from the still empty car park wondering whether they would be serving tea at the Mill. It might be interesting to see inside. But then he decided it all looked too upscale for "teas" and they would be preparing for dinners. He was ready to go home. When he got to the hotel, however, it was already too late to call British Airways about changing his tickets.

CHAPTER 12

That evening he went to the bar, looking for company, straight after dinner (the cold "lamb salad" was not a success). The room was almost empty, so he took a stool directly in front of the barman.

"It was whiskey, wasn't it?"

"If you please, and a little soda perhaps."

The bartender brought the glass and a tall soda siphon but did not offer the ice bucket.

"You'll be here on business?"

"No, I'm just here for a quiet visit, a sort of vaca... (he caught himself) holiday."

"That's nice. We don't get many Yanks, pardon, Americans, taking their holidays here. It's quiet at this time of year, kiddies still in school till this week Come to think of it, it's always quiet, except for the fair, first week in November."

"Do they still have the fair?"

"Ay, happen they do. But wait, tha's been here before then." The bartender was surprised, and his voice picked up more of a local inflexion.

"I used to live here when I was a boy. Haven't been back since, but I remember the fair."

"Get on! Tha' was at the Grammar School then?"

"Yes, seems a long time ago, but the town hasn't changed much."

"Never changes, this place. What years?"

"At school?"

"Aye."

"I left in 1960 after the sixth form."

"Oh ay. I left in 1965 but were only 16. Couldn't stand that sixth-form stuff. You must have been there same time as me then. Just. What's yer name, if you don't mind my asking."

"Philip Halliday. I'm afraid I don't remember you."

"Fred Lakin, Cottisthorpe born and bred. Left school to work for me dad and then joined the army. Been here at the White Horse for nigh on 15 year. Well, fancy you being at the school too. I don't remember you either, but we've all changed summat awful."

He went down to the end of the bar to rearrange some cases of wine or spirits. Philip stayed where he was, wondering if it would be rude, now, to retire to a table.

"Who were some of the others in your form then?" Fred was working his way back down the bar.

"I've been trying to remember. Alan Sharpe, Malcolm

someone or other, father was a grocer. Richard Evans, his father taught at the elementary school."

"Ay, died long since, did Alan. Great lummox, got as fat as an ox. You can guess what happened to him." Philip couldn't (didn't remember Alan as fat).

"Heart attack, wasn't it? And Malcolm went off to London. Did ye know Ed Clemerson, played rugby, he did."

"The name seems familiar."

"Aye. Died in a car accident these ten years back."

"He had a sister, I think."

"Married and left. They most have, tha' knows. Anyone as finished sixth form and specially the university; they never came back here to live. All your mates, I don't doubt. And the older folks too, retired and moved south. Nothing much to stay here for, is there? Where did you live, then?"

"Stacey Street, just round the corner, I'm afraid."

"Aye, y've seen it, then. Big changes there!"

"The town looks prosperous, now."

"Aye, these last ten years farming has taken off. Land's worth a bomb and the farmers are getting rich. Which there's no jobs, though. Minton's was taken over and a lot of it is shut down. There's new building over Nottingham way. Some work there, for the moment anyway. But there's loads of unemployed here, though, especially the immigrants. The shops are empty, and the market tomorrow will be crammed with folks looking for summat cheap. You don't see many of the lads spending freely in here tonight, do you?"

By now Philip was on his second whiskey. He offered Fred Lakin a beer and they drank in silence for a while. Fred seemed perfectly happy to stand and polish the bar top.

"Don't mind me, this'd drive yer mad, remembering old names from the Dark Ages, but do you mind old Mr. Allen, the math teacher? He's still around, nigh on 85 I reckon, and drives the same old car – blue Morris Minor – as ever. I often see him."

"I'll look for him, although I'll probably be leaving in the next day or so." Philip hesitated. "Did you know Neil Holyroyd?"

"Oh, aye, Neil. That's right. He'd be about your age. Went to Australia, you know. Took his mam with him. Older than me, but his brother, John, *he's* here. I know him. Everyone knows John. It'll not be long before you bump into him. In here, most like."

Just then two older women (60s to 70s) came in and Fred greeted them cheekily.

"Hello girls, out on the town again are we?"

Philip took his chance and with a quick "thanks" moved to a table to finish his whiskey.

He was deep in thought, remembering again the afternoons spent train spotting when the barman sat down next to him. Philip looked up to see that the bar was almost empty; everyone had left except the two women who had just come in, and a scruffy old man staring into a half-pint glass of beer.

"Quiet tonight. I was thinking, what did your dad do?"

"He was manager of the bank, Barclays, and then he got moved down to London."

"So you didn't live here very long then. What attracted you to come back then, after all these years, if you don't mind me asking." He was being circumspect and was using less of the local twang.

Despite his intention to leave, this conversation with Lakin had intrigued Philip. So he plunged in, although he had decided not to. Trouble was, he couldn't just spend time here poking around without some kind of a reason. Not in a small town like this.

"Well, I've been thinking of doing some writing…"

He had decided on this "cover" in Philadelphia. And it was partly true: if he ever left the firm, he would love to become a writer, but of what?

"Nothing very serious, but I had an idea for writing something that would include Cottisthorpe – back thirty years, that is."

"Oh aye, like a travel book you mean?"

Fred's manner had changed subtly, and Philip immediately regretted having brought up such a silly idea.

"Nothing much to write about here. Quiet as one of them ghost towns. Even more when you was here. I don't think that would wash. You want a bit of excitement, but."

"I know. I know. Nothing ever happened when I was here, although there was a man murdered, I remember, about the time I left. No, I was thinking of things in the historical line. The history of the town, farming, the mills, and so on." He felt his voice shaking slightly. He had tried to be so casual... "a man murdered." It felt as though he had just blurted it out.

"Well, I don't like to contradict, but there was nothing like that here."

"Sorry, like what."

Fred, looking bleak, leaned forward.

"What you just said – 'murder' – not here in Cottisthorpe. Yer probably remembering summat from the papers, somewhere else. I were old enough then to know. There was no murder here. You're wasting your time I'm afraid. Nottingham or London, that's where you'd best be."

Philip said nothing, surprised by Fred's response.

The barman looked over his shoulder and called to the man at the bar. "Hey, Wiggy! There's never been a man murdered in Cottisthorpe, has there? Back nearly 25 years?"

The man looked up and scowled. Philip could see that he lacked most of his teeth.

"Naw! Who th'ell wants to know?"

"Listen to old Wiggy. We're quiet here you know. Folks might not appreciate it if you try to write as though they'd been summat like that going on here. Best to let it drop."

"Well, as I said, it's the history I'm interested in."

Fred's face was troubled. "Aye. Ye'd be on the wrong track, my son. I should forget the whole thing."

Philip bristled at the familiar, patronizing, "my son"

from a younger man, but he seemed to mean well. He was probably right in every sense. He quickly made his excuses and headed off to bed, taking the steps two at a time. He would call the airline tomorrow.

As he left, Wiggy looked up quickly from his beer, while Fred Larkin watched until the door closed, and even then, had a deep frown.

CHAPTER 13

A tiny ripple of anxiety started to spread in the little country town. The schoolteacher's phone rang at 6:45 am. She swore mildly to herself as she padded downstairs to answer – thinking yet again how useful it would be to have a telephone in her bedroom. Not that it rang all that often.

After listening for a few moments, she put the receiver down without a word and then sat on the stairs to think. What was all this, and why now? Damn, school had just ended, and she was looking forward to a real rest. Why did this have to happen now? And who put *him* in charge, anyway?

By 8:30 she had parked her car on a side street near the center of town, finding a spot just before the market day crowds filled the town center completely. Then she started carefully following her instructions, which turned out to be absurdly easy, at first.

The police sergeant was feeling confident, too. This

situation could be handled easily, no need to panic. But he reported it higher up, just in case. They seemed surprisingly relaxed. No problem, they said, you can sort that.

The old man in his cottage by the canal was drunk and probably would be for a day or so. A friend had given him a half-full bottle of the good stuff last night and he had wasted no time drinking most of it. Good chap he was, always had been even if he came across as a bit superior sometimes. Not like his dad, that bastard.

CHAPTER 14

Philip lay in bed trying to decide whether to try to get up and dress before Mrs. Henslow arrived with tea. Which would be worse: being served tea in bed again, or having her arrive while he was dressing? Would she mind if he asked her to leave it in the hall outside the door? He was still cursing himself for having forgotten to cancel the tea altogether when the inevitable knock came, followed by a panting Queenie Henslow.

"Here you are, Mr. Halliday. Oh, what a rush it is today!"

Then she hurried out, panting with effort, leaving Philip to sip anxiously on the sweet, hot tea and register with half his brain that the parking lot outside the window seemed to be very busy this sunny morning.

Despite everything, he felt curiously more relaxed. Even if he got a plane back as soon as possible it would probably take a couple of days. Meanwhile, he might as well keep looking around, visit the library perhaps, and he really ought to explore the countryside better; find some good bird-watching spots. There had been some lovely churches in the small neighboring towns. A place called Staunton Harold had a church that was memorable for something-or-other. Perhaps he would start to meet people he knew. Perhaps! On such a pretty morning. And he would feel much better when he got over the jet lag.

The small dining room was full. Philip hesitated in the doorway, slightly embarrassed, but Mrs. Henslow pushed forward out of a group of middle-aged ladies and greeted him.

"Here you are then. Doreen will find you a place."

As Doreen came out of the kitchen followed by the tall boy, at once it was clear that they were all one family: grandma, mother, and grandson.

"Ooh, it's ever so crowded this morning. You'll have to share a table, do you mind?"

This was not really a question. Not giving him any chance to mind, she led him to a table for two at which an elderly man was just finishing a plate that had once held a herculean pile of eggs, sausages, and bacon. Remnants of toast were scattered all around. There was just time to notice that his sweater was old, but good quality and well darned. As Philip started to clear his throat to say something in greeting, the old man grabbed his teacup, shot down what remained in it, and almost ran for the door. He never once lifted his eyes to look at him.

"Always in a rush, that one," Doreen said from behind

him, reaching for the dirty plates. "And what an appetite. That's why I put you here, I knew he'd soon be gone."

"Looked like an interesting man."

Doreen looked at him for a moment to see if this was sarcasm. "I suppose. He has three stalls in the market. Gets them set up first and then leaves his sons to watch things while he comes in here for breakfast. He even pays first so he won't have to wait for the bill. Has the same thing every time, doesn't he?"

"Every week?"

"Twice a week. Market days, Thursday, and Saturday."

She was saying "market." Finally, it dawned on him. It was Thursday. "So they still have the market?"

Doreen looked at him as though he were crazy. "Of course they have the market!"

At least that hadn't changed. Suddenly he wanted very much to see the market again, probably the same market that had been conducted here for 700 years. But first, there was breakfast.

"What would you like, then? That cereal?" There was a note of disdain in her voice.

"No, Doreen, bring me what he had. Well, just the eggs."

"Good for you. Be right up. I'll bring your tea first."

"Would you have any orange juice?"

Doreen's face fell – just as she had started to please him!

"There might be one of those little bottles in the bar, I could look."

"No, never mind. Just bring the tea."

She stood there, uncertain.

"Tea'll be just great. Won't it." He tried a big smile and Doreen went off happily. The trick of communicating in Cottisthorpe, he decided, was to end every sentence with a question – wasn't it?

He wasn't really sure how he could eat the huge plate of scrambled eggs when it appeared, let alone the fried tomatoes. But they went down quickly, and he sat in the rapidly emptying room with an odd feeling of contentment. And there was the market to look forward to.

It was just the same. Exactly. The empty square at the center of town was now filled with two rows of market stalls, each made of canvas set upon poles that fitted (it was all coming back) into the metal sockets let into the pavement. The town workmen set them up and took them down and the tradespeople rented them, some surely passed down continuously within the family for generations. The stalls sold everything from meat and fish to vegetables, flowers, and cheap clothing, especially shoes. Many simply sold cloth materials for dressmaking: linens, and such. One sold pure knick-knacks in china and cheaper metal, some had pots and pans; others sold second-hand records and tapes. A pony-tailed young man was selling upscale herbs and watercolors. A few stalls were vacant.

He wandered up and down the long row happily, all the while scanning faces for anyone familiar. It was like all street markets around the world, Exmouth Market in central London or the market on Sundays near the Bastille in Paris. Cheap, lively, noisy, and colorful.

One change made it even more cosmopolitan and gave it even more the air of the medieval markets that had preceded it. Amidst the colorful wares for sale were garishly colored fabrics from perhaps a dozen countries in Asia, Africa, and the Caribbean. Slender women in saris manned stalls and handsome women in tie-dyed dashikis bought vegetables. But Philip soon found himself stopping in pure amazement. From the mouths of these gloriously diverse people and their energetic children came exactly the same broad, flat, East Midlands voices as from the English who had been there long before. If he were to close his eyes, it would be one voice, the voice of the markets of his youth.

In a sense, it was all wrong. They should speak their own way, with their own lilting phrases, those characteristic Indian and Caribbean cadences – not this flatland dullness. But it was also wonderfully right. These people were thoroughly integrated into this society. They spoke like this because they had been born here and gone to school here. They hadn't tried to keep their voices different.

Philip worked his way twice through the market and now started to look for somewhere to get coffee. Here at the wide southern end of the Market Square, where the remnants of a 17th-century butter cross formed a small traffic island, stood the police sergeant again, the same one as yesterday. He stood there almost like a caricature of the old English Bobby, hands behind his back, watching the crowd. Philip caught his eye; there seemed nothing to do but nod, so he did, and the policeman gravely nodded back – really just lowered the peak of his helmet just a fraction. The gesture said, "I've seen you. I've already registered you. I'm in charge."

Flushed and angry, Philip hurried on. Now the jostling crowds irritated him, perhaps because they all seemed so poor and – worse – the English seemed so indifferent to their appearance and their manners. The only really interesting thing about the market, with its cheap wares and strong smells of cabbage and fish, was its integration.

He could feel that the policeman's eyes were still on his back. He found a coffee shop next door to the camera place, so first stopped in for film and then went and sat at a table to drink easily the worst coffee he had ever tasted. He pushed aside the cup, half-finished, and headed for the library having forgotten to call the airline.

CHAPTER 15

Nothing much had changed here. The main room of the library was still the reading room, with rows of wooden bookshelves on both sides. He walked over to the left and peered at the books. This is where "literature" had been in his day and where, one memorably rainy summer, he had read his way through all of Dostoevsky not really retaining very much, mostly just reading it because it was there. Only a short walk from his house, the library was always open, warm, and inviting. And quiet.

The new building connected with this big room, and he saw that it was largely a children's library with modern furnishings, especially computers, of course. Soft cushions lay about the floor, in bright colors sharply contrasting with the timeless oak charm of the old reading room.

However, the library was not at all quiet. School must have ended, because there were many children – come to think of it, there had been children in the market, too – and neither they nor the several adults in the main reading room area were being particularly respectful of the old library rule – "silence." In a way, it was nicer. Everyone here was enjoying themselves.

A very young woman at the circulation desk, perhaps only a teenager, caught his eye and he stepped forward.

"I was wondering if you have a back file of the local newspapers, for the 1950s and 1960s, actually."

"Oh, no. We don't keep old papers. Just for a month."

"No, I mean, on file. There must be a microfilm or something, for reference."

She looked at him somewhat belligerently, started to say "no" again, then stopped and disappeared through a door behind. He wondered whether he should leave but, after a moment, an older woman came out with her.

"Good morning, you're looking for reference materials?"

This must be the town librarian, very much in charge.

"Yes, please, I think you'd call it reference. I wanted to look through local papers for the late 50s and early 60s."

"Yes, we have everything on microfiche. Which paper did you want?"

"Ah, well! Let me think. Back then it was the weekly *Reporter*, I think."

"*Reporter* on Friday mornings, *Record* on Tuesdays, in the afternoon. They merged in 1969."

He blinked. "Oh, yes, confusing names – the *Record*

was a tabloid, and the *Reporter* was full-sized. Do you have both?"

As if this seemed too greedy a request, the woman obviously thought for a second before answering.

"Yes, we do."

"Then I think I'd like to start with the years 1957 to 1961 if that is alright."

"What sort of research are you doing, if you don't mind my asking?"

"Oh dear. It's nothing that fancy. I used to live here and just wanted to look back over names and places from those days."

"You're a writer, then?"

"Oh, well, I've written a couple of small books on finance."

"I wonder if we have anything of yours?" Her voice made it sound as though this was extremely doubtful.

"Philip Halliday is my name. I'm sure not; they are quite technical and published in America, as you could no doubt guess."

"Well, I suppose you'd better come with me. The microfiche reader is in the office."

Something in her shoulders told Philip that casual curiosity was discouraged here. However, she took him through the door behind the desk into a large room, clearly original to the building. It was a combination storeroom and office area, full to overflowing with books and file boxes but somehow still looked highly organized.

"I'm Miss Henderson. Do you mind signing our register?"

It was an order anyway.

As he signed, he asked, "I have this odd feeling that the old librarian – in my day that is – was a Mr. Henderson. Was...?"

"...my father, yes." She smiled.

"Well, that's wonderful. He was very kind to me, I used to almost live here in those days."

"Yes? I went away to boarding school, so never saw much of things here then. He's retired now, moved to Eastbourne, and I've been the Borough Librarian for 10 years. Now, let's get on. Do you know how to work a reader like this?"

"Oh, yes. I've worked one pretty much like this. Shouldn't be a problem."

He switched it on and checked the controls while she watched for a moment and then went over to a cupboard.

"We don't often get a call for these. Let's see. Oh..." She stopped, slightly flushed, and thought.

"Yes, I remember now, the year 1961 is missing."

She brought over some small envelopes.

"It is missing for both papers. Someone must have borrowed them and not returned them, I'm sorry."

Sitting at the desk, with the familiar prospect of "looking things up," he relaxed a little. First, he flipped through the front pages. Most of the town's weekly news meant nothing to him at all – records of Council meetings and decisions long since redundant, traffic accidents, visits from very minor royalty for the usual sorts of civic functions (never the Queen or Queen Mother, not even Princess Margaret – those he would have remembered.) But then when he started on the inside pages, a lot of memories started flooding back. He couldn't resist looking for his own name in the sports sections – and there in the summer of 1958, he found it for the first time. The box score of a cricket match which the school had lost. He hadn't done very well: two wickets for 27 runs.

Names of friends, or more often their parents, started to show up and advertisements for stores that he remembered; several references to his father when he started a fund for the Red Cross to relieve the victims of a mine disaster in South Yorkshire. All the history of the town was laid out and he started to read slower and slower.

Those had indeed been quiet years. So Fred Larkin and his friend Wiggy had been right. Except that the year 1961 was missing. That had been his last year in Cottisthorpe.

Once he finished 1960, he decided to break for lunch, telling Miss Henderson that he would probably be back, so not to put the films away, "if that was alright, of course." As he left, he noticed a very attractive woman sitting in the reading room. She seemed to be looking at him. He wondered briefly if it was someone who recognized him from the old days, but she looked away too quickly. Probably she had heard his American accent and was curious. Too bad, she was very handsome, with wonderful dark hair showing red highlights.

When he came back, the librarian left him to work in

the office all alone, evidently having decided he was safe. He went back carefully through the years but got nowhere. The young girl wandered in every now and again. At 3:30 he was about to give up when she appeared and rather awkwardly asked him if he would like a cup of tea. When he accepted, she looked rather relieved, and then he saw why. This was also the staff tearoom.

The girl – Eileen, she shyly announced – filled an electric kettle from a sink in the corner and soon sat down opposite him with tea and some sweet biscuits after taking a cup to the redoubtable Miss Henderson, working in some other room.

"Is it interesting then, what you're finding? You've been ever so quiet."

"Well, yes, it is. It's fascinating. You see I lived here and was at the school, so in addition to seeing all the history of the town, I keep finding references to people I knew well and even to myself – just school sports, of course."

"I wasn't born til 1970."

"Well, you should look up those years, I bet there's a birth announcement your parents put in, at least."

"Yes, there would be, wouldn't there. But are you looking for something special? In boring old Cottisthorpe?"

"Well, you're right. There's not much here. Very dull Cottisthorpe was then."

"Still is, if you ask me. I'm off as soon as I finish this internship..."

She stopped guiltily as Miss Henderson came in,

clearly expressing disapproval that he was sitting having tea with the staff. Eileen cleared the cups away.

Philip wondered if there was any point in looking at 1962 or later. He hadn't been in Cottisthorpe in 1962 – or the last half of 1961 for that matter. It was too far afield: not worth looking there. Or was it? He had time, so why not?

"One thing, Miss Henderson, would it be too much trouble to look for the microfiches for 1962?" He was learning the right phrasing. "I imagine I've just got time for one more year."

Miss Henderson produced 1962 without hesitation, putting the others carefully away.

Philip went through the *Reporter* first, page by page. Until he came to the second week of October. On the front page was a large article noting the anniversary of the death in 1961 of a small girl named Angela Hand, nine years old. She had been strangled and left dead in a shed in a field off the Derby Road. A shed!

"That's wrong!" His chair shifted and he put out his hand, knocking over some boxes. It had been a man, not a girl.

The girl Eileen came over cautiously.

"Mr. Halliday, did you say something?"

"Oh, yes, I must be talking to myself now. What next?" He tried a smile.

"It's probably from staring down that reader for hours on end."

Miss Henderson, at a desk on the other side of the room, looked over curiously.

He stood up and took a few steps around the room. This was very confusing. He remembered it quite well, now. He had been in his first month or so at Durham and there had been stuff in the papers, but he hadn't paid much attention. Too busy starting out as a freshman, perhaps. Yes, there had been a murder of a little girl. Not a man. He'd been wrong.

"Got to clear my head."

There had been a murder after all. But nothing like the one in his dream.

The younger woman – Eileen – had moved behind him and pretty surely had glanced down at the screen as she went by.

Philip sat and read on.

"...strangled in a garden shed on Derby Road at the end of Prince William Street, near the railway level-crossing."

The *Record* had the same story but in a longer treatment. He read with terrible fascination the reason for the story: the murder was unsolved. A whole year, the paper rumbled, and no arrests. There was a statement from the Chief Constable but nothing from the victim's parents. The more he read, the more curious he became.

He went back to the *Reporter* and read on, week after week. Until he came to the third week in December. Now the little girl's mother had also died. Complications from pneumonia. This time more of the original story came out. Now there was a very clear hint that the child had been sexually molested. She had strayed from home after school and was not found until the evening of the following day. The time of death had been fixed at some time between 4:00 and 8:00 pm. The police had no suspects at the time and had none since. Upset neighbors were interviewed and said that the loss of the little girl was what had really killed Mrs. Hand, herself only 35. There was an older sister who was not living with relatives.

The girl was said to have been friendly and trusting, used to walking up to the corner shop by herself, and running errands for her mother. The family had lived in Newcastle Street, not a hundred yards from where the body was found in a shed in the back of a garden. No one had seen anything unusual. The father had been at work, the mother at home all day.

As he read on, his panic subsided. For a moment he had been sure that he must somehow have committed this murder himself – it was the murder in his dream. But as the details unfolded, confused as he was, he knew that was absurd. Nothing had any shade of familiarity; he had been a student, for God's sake, miles away. Nothing of this had anything to do with him.

The more he read, the more he remembered. It had been in the national papers which he had read at Durham. With the connection to Cottisthorpe, of course he had read it. Had his parents written to him about it? Perhaps not, his father would have found it all highly distasteful.

Miss Henderson said, "How is it going? I'm afraid I shall have to put you out soon, so as we can close up."

"Oh dear. Well, yes. That's fine. I haven't really got very far."

"Were you looking for a terrible scandal or something like that?"

"Scandal would have been good: the mayor running off with the headmistress of the high school, or Archdeacon West borrowing from the vestry fund to fuel a gambling habit." Philip knew he was trying too hard.

The librarian looked at him very coolly, with pursed lips. "I'm sure you won't find anything like that here in Cottisthorpe. That's more what they get up to in America, isn't it."

CHAPTER 16

He ate dinner quietly, not really hungry, just going through the motions. Trying to bring back long-forgotten details. Trying not to admit his underlying terror. He had known about this child's murder, all those years ago, but had somehow suppressed it in his preoccupation with his dreams about a man being murdered. But it was peculiar that there had been a murder after all. When he had asked about a murder, Fred had been insistent, vehement almost, that there had been no murder. Fred and that other chap, too.

He tried to think logically. He had asked them about "the murder of a man." So technically, Fred had been right. But it had been idle conversation in a bar, not a court of law. And Fred and been so fierce. And, in retrospect, rather anxious to get rid of him. It didn't make sense. Unless, of course, the locals were very sensitive about that child's murder. Perhaps it was still unsolved. But would that account for Fred having more or less directly told him to go home and mind his own business? Twenty-five years had gone by.

Given Fred's manner, it was probably no coincidence that the microfiches for the year of the murder were missing from the library. The locals wanted to discourage anyone from enquiring about that murder. Which made it a challenge. It would be very interesting to try to find out more. Perhaps the big, central library in Nottingham would have the missing local newspapers, and the national papers, for October 1961.

After dinner, he really felt as though he needed a drink or two or he would have no chance of sleeping. And he was very curious to talk to Fred Lakin again. But the bar was crowded and Fred was quite busy. A large TV set had been moved to a corner of the bar and a soccer match was in progress. He sat at a table with a trial glass of the local bitter. It seemed more appropriate for a soccer game than whiskey.

The game was evidently between two European teams, but he couldn't discover which. The game was already in progress and the announcer didn't bother with the names of the teams, having his hands full (or mouth, really) with the names of the players.

Halliday watched idly, starting to recite to himself, with growing pleasure, some of the names of the great European teams whose football then, as now, apparently (judging from the comments of the announcer), was slicker and more technical than the English game: Real Madrid, Juventus, Moscow Dynamo, Red Star, Ajax... there were other names. What were those wonderful Scottish teams...Hearts of Midlothian, Dundee Athletic, Dunfermline, Partick Thistle?

In his reverie, the flashing images of the football match largely unseen, he was completely unaware of being approached.

"I reckon you don't remember me?"

It was a question rather than a statement. Philip turned to find himself looking at the belt buckle of the large police sergeant, now with a tweed sports jacket over his blue shirt, black tie, and black uniform trousers. The man sat down without being invited.

"You're Philip Halliday. I thought I recognized you day 'afore yesterday, so I checked Queenie's book. You'll not remember me, then?"

"I'm terribly sorry..."

"It's John, John Holyroyd."

"Good heavens, Neil's brother!" He almost said, "little brother" but one could see how the chubby little boy had grown, and then grown some more. "For heavens' sake. That's great. How are you?"

"What brings you back here, then?"

Philip's mind was elsewhere. This was the policeman he had been seeing everywhere, but he was Neil's brother. Why hadn't he introduced himself before?

"You're Neil's brother. I understand he went to Australia?"

"Neil? Aye. Couldn't stand it there, though, no more than here. He's a schoolteacher in Ireland now, just outside Dublin."

"Dublin, how odd!"

"Not really. He married an Irish lass. She's got family there. We've none here. That is, I'm here and my wife and kiddies, but there's no one else."

"Your mother?" Philip could see her smiling at the kitchen table, fussing over her boys, keeping them out of the way of the erratic and dangerous father.

"Died these fifteen years since. She went to Aussie with our Neil and died there. Cancer, she had. Had it all along; we just didn't know. But she loved our Neil, and he wanted her to go with him."

"I'm sorry. She was a lovely person. I remember her so well. She was always laughing, always spoiling us."

"She was that." But his voice was cold, defensive, saying, "She was my mother, you keep your distance."

"And you, you've been here all along?"

"The National Service call-up ended, you know, but I'd always thought I'd be a soldier, so I signed up. Four years. They put me in the Military Police, then I got out and joined this lot. Came back here and have been here ever since. I'm a sergeant now. I'll never leave here; they'd have to shoot me. Now, are you staying long?"

"Just a few days."

"Right."

Without warning, he got up.

I'll leave you to your drink. Expect I'll see you again before you go."

Had Philip offended him, he wondered. The man left so abruptly. Had it been rude not to answer about why he was here? If he had stayed, Philip could have asked him about the little girl's murder.

CHAPTER 17

Trained as an historian, Philip now had something he could deal with. By 10:30 the next morning, he was ensconced in the main public library in Nottingham. This time, getting access to the microfiche files had been a little more difficult. He had to sign in and give identification, state his reasons for wanting to see the material, and sign a form promising to observe copyrights and generally behave like a Christian. But they let him sit in a large reference room and work his way steadily through the national papers for October 1961.

At first, he seemed to be learning nothing much new. The local papers had covered it pretty well in their "One-Year Anniversary of Kiddie Horror" stories. There were more photographs and a small amount of extra information about the family. The father, William Gregory Hand, had worked in Minton's cotton mill, along with almost every other male who lived in the bottom half of the town. The mother didn't work, of course, it being 1961. The older sister was 15 at the time.

After plowing through the overlapping accounts, Philip was about to give up when he noticed an almost offhand remark in the *News Chronicle* (a national daily, now long extinct) of October 23, 1962. ".... This brutal and senseless tragedy which echoes the murder of Anne Dexter at Wigstall in 1952."

Wigstall was a suburb of Leicester, some 35 miles from Cottisthorpe. On a whim, Philip asked for the microfiche for the Leicester paper for 1952. To his surprise, the library didn't carry the Leicester papers for that period. But he found a good deal of information in the Nottingham one anyway and, again, the nationals. It was even more shocking.

December 10th, 1951: Ann Dexter had been nine years old when she disappeared one evening and was found four days later, strangled in a shed on an allotment. She had been sexually molested. Ten days later a friend of the family, one William Green, had been charged with the murder. Green had a criminal record for interfering with young children as a minor with two years in a "home," and also a deferred sentence for shoplifting. He had been in the vicinity of the Dexter house on the fateful day. On February 4th, 1952, Green was found guilty of the murder of Ann Dexter and three months weeks later he was hanged in Leicester jail.

When Philip looked at his watch, it turned out to be 3:30 already. Asking at the main desk, he got directions to a cafe and sat down to eat a cheese sandwich and drink a cup of strong coffee. Back at the library, he scanned the years as fast as he could – there was no notice of an arrest for Angela Hand's murder.

CHAPTER 18

Next morning, at Leicester's main library, Philip sat down with all the accounts he could find of both the 1952 and 1961 murders, knowing what he would find – a night without sleeping had made it clear.

They were identical. Anyone could see that. Of course, he didn't know how many other murders of little girls (or boys and girls) there might have been across the country in that period. But the coincidence here was too great.

However, the murderer of the first little girl had been caught. He had long been dead when the second murder occurred. Was it a copycat crime? Must have been. Unless, of course, there was a second possibility. Suppose Green had been the wrong man? Had the wrong man been hanged for the Dexter murder in 1951? The first murderer would still have been at large, to strike again in another town. But surely the police would have seen that. Surely the police had investigated the similarity between the two cases.

Hell, if he had seen the similarity, anyone could have. Which of course, explained Cottisthorpe people being sensitive on the subject. But even so, it was decades ago. What were they still covering up? This was both terrible and exciting. He knew he couldn't go home without doing more research. The historian in him wouldn't allow it. And more than that, he still needed to know if there was any connection between these two murders and his dreams.

One point of approach was available: he had passed through Wigstall on his way into Leicester. He could get a map and try to find the district where the first girl had been killed. Perhaps there would be someone around who still remembered. It was worth a try. Why not?

The newspapers said that the allotments had been behind Castleview Street, a strange name since there was no castle to see. The library's map showed Castleview running parallel to the main road with an open space that might still be the allotments between the two. The best approach seemed to be to go past and then turn onto Mayhew, then back on to Castleview. Easy.

And in fact, it was even easier. As he approached Mayhew, he saw the familiar green sign for a public footpath pointing down a broad path between the houses. Surely that led to the allotments. He turned the car at the next intersection, looking for a place to park. Just up ahead there was a small pull-off (lay-by, they would call it) about a hundred yards up. So he left the car and walked back.

The path led between high, unfriendly fences obviously put there by the local council. In ugly concrete, they were much more substantial than fitted the houses of the area – a mixture of semi-detached and four-in-a-row. Most of the houses had no garages and their front gardens had been paved over with stones or tarmac to make parking spaces. But some had wonderful gardens, with bright, if rather formal, rows of dahlias, asters, and every kind of annual.

Following the path, he saw the allotments open up to his right. There were perhaps six acres of open land, divided into separate plots, each distinguished from the others by a different arrangement of compost piles, bean poles, rubbish bins, and tidy rows of vegetables. There was something quintessentially English about this scene. The smell of earth and compost, the organized plots of land, all different but basically the same. The tiny scale: each plot was only about 15 by 30 feet. Somehow, he found it very claustrophobic. Each plot here was a doll-sized farm, with a field and barn. In fact, each was a little empire to some man or other (this was not a woman's world).

With a shiver, he saw that many of the plots also had sheds, small affairs to keep tools in. Some were plastic, most were galvanized metal. Only one was wood. There were even two small greenhouses. All were shabby and much-patched together, rather amateurishly.

He thought of the two little girls, both murdered in garden sheds, sheds like these. And probably just like the one on the meadows where he and Neil had played. Presumably, one of these was actually where Anne Dexter had been killed.

Off to the left, an old man, dressed in dark trousers and an old-fashioned dress shirt without a collar, sleeves rolled up, was working on a row of what might be onions, or leeks more likely. Philip picked his way between the plots, while the man kept working. He looked up only at the last moment.

"Good morning."

The man replied cautiously, "Aye!"

"I wonder if I could speak to you for a moment."

"Whatever it is, I don't want it."

"No, I'm not selling anything."

The man narrowed his eyes.

"You're a Yank, Canadian, what?"

"I live in America, but I was brought up here, or rather, over in Cottisthorpe."

"Oh, aye." It was a dubious response as if Cottisthorpe were under quarantine.

"Did you live here in 1951?"

"'51 you say. You'll be a reporter, then. Long time since we've had you lot around."

Here, perhaps, his "cover" would actually be useful. "Sorry, yes, I am; well, sort of. I'm writing a book, and I wanted to ask about the Dexter murder. It must have been somewhere here."

"It were," the old man said, not moving a muscle.

"I'd be willing to pay you for your time, of course," said Philip in a moment of inspiration.

"Oh, aye."

Philip gave him a 20-pound note. Neither spoke, and then the man pointed off down the slope.

"Down there, it was. All gone now. Shed and all. It's houses now. There's nothing to see. Nothing there."

"You were here then?"

"Aye, moved here in 1948. Joe Towles and his sons, and the Wilsons, and that Bob French. All of us."

"The dead girl's family too."

"That's what I said."

The old man spat, "he were from Leicester, but he mostly stayed with his mates, a few streets over."

"Do you think he was guilty?"

The old man suddenly became angry.

"Of course he were. What d'ye think? They hanged him, didn't they?"

"But the case was weak."

"Naw! Any road up, the rope were thick. Bad lot, all of them."

"All who?"

That Green and his pals. None of them worth a penny. Always in trouble. In the nick half the time."

"And now."

"They've all gone, long since, bad cess to 'em."

"Including the girl's family?"

"Ah, they was alright, she were just a wee one. But her

mam had no business leaving her all the time. Asking for trouble. Too busy hanging around the George to take care of the little mite."

"Did William Green hang around the pub, too?"

"Yer askin' a lot o' questions!"

The old man looked expectantly. Another 20 was produced.

"Of course. That's how they knew who to look for. The little girl's dad told the police Green had done it."

"The father."

"Or mebbe one of the other lads; I don't rightly remember."

"So the case was easy then."

"Arrested within the week, weren't he? Hung not three month later." Another spit.

"Are *any* of the people you mentioned still around?"

"Nay, all gone."

"Green had been arrested before for molesting children."

"Aye, so they say."

The old man hesitated.

"Yes?"

"Between 'em all, no kid was safe."

"You mean..."

"I've said all I will and more than I should. You'd best be off, I've me work to do."

"Did you hear about another murder, in Cottisthorpe, about ten years later?"

The old man bent over to plant again.

"You'd best be going."

Philip made his way back across the allotment to the path trying carefully to recall everything the old man had said.

The main road was relatively deserted. A dark blue car was parked further down the hill and a bus roared past, spewing diesel fumes. About halfway back to the car, Philip heard an engine close behind him, almost too close. He half turned, just as there was a bump and a car came straight towards him, having mounted the curb. Philip leapt to the side and feet against a hedge as the car roared past. He had just a second to see that it was brown and older looking. He would never have recognized the model anyway.

He picked himself up carefully as another car drew alongside and a youngish man, full of indignation looked over.

"Hey, are you alright? Perhaps you should sit down, you may be hurt."

"No, I think I'm fine. I got out of the way. I twisted my ankle a bit."

"It was some old chap – shouldn't be driving at his age. He could have killed you. Too many old folks driving.

"Did you get the plate number?"

"Sorry, no. Are you alright?"

"Yes, look, my car's just over there. I'm fine. Thank you very much. I appreciate it."

He looked over his shoulder and saw the blue car still parked lower down on the slope. A woman stood beside it, her hands to her mouth in a gesture, even at this distance he could tell, of fear.

Philip stood as the man drove off, and then limped back to his car. Before he started the engine, though, the thought struck him. "Old feller!" He hobbled back to the allotments.

"That old bastard had better still be there. If he tried to run me down..."

But there was the old man, bent over in the distance, cleaning his hoe with a rag.

CHAPTER 19

That evening, John Holyroyd was already sitting at a table in the bar when Philip came in from the dining room. Holyroyd got up and gestured for him to come over.

"What'll yer have? Oh, this is the wife, Marian."

Marian was indeed the woman he had seen John Holyroyd with on the first evening. She was friendly-looking with a slightly sad smile and bleached blond hair. She should have been behind the bar instead of Fred.

"I gather you're an old friend of John's then, Mr. Halliday."

"Please call me Philip. Yes, although to be accurate, I was a friend of Neil's."

"Neil's a good man."

John came with the whiskey. Philip realized that he should have asked for beer – cheaper.

They chatted for a while. Marian was a genuinely nice person and very anxious to make Philip feel at home.

Philip warmed to her immediately and soon learned a great deal about their two children, and Marian's mother in a nursing home, which reminded him that he was curious about John's father.

"What about your father," he asked John. Is he still living?"

"What about him? Oh, well, I can tell you. If I don't someone else will. He died long since. Fact is, Fred here's dad ran him over with his lorry, in East Gate. You remember him, I can tell. Well, after our Neil went off to the Polytechnic in Liverpool, he got a lot worse."

"I know he used to beat you and Neil, and frankly, I wondered if he hit your mother too."

"Did you now? Well, he did. He hit me most. Neil was his favorite, but when he did hit him, it were real hard. And as for me, he'd pull off that belt for almost anything. I could never do anything right. That's why I left home as soon as I could, and that's why Neil took our mam off to Australia when he moved out there. We talked about it all the time. He didn't want to leave me alone with our dad, and he didn't want to leave mam with him. So we all three packed it in together."

"What happened then?"

"Nothing much at first, then he really started ranting and raving on Jesus. No, I tell a lie; it started earlier. As soon as Neil'd left for Liverpool he'd stand in the street at all hours preaching, as he called it. Shouting more like. He'd walk up and down the market shouting that he was a terrible sinner, we were all terrible sinners, and the Lord would come and punish us, punish the whole town. Cottisthorpe were the new Sodom and Gomorrah. The world would come to an end. Stuff like that. Anyway, he started doing it at work, so they gave him the boot.

"The worst thing was, he took a lot of mam's savings and hired the old butcher's down on the Nottingham Road, just this side of the canal, and set up what he called his Church of Christ's Holy Word. Summat like that. Great on the Holy Bloody Word, he was.

"That was the last straw, you see, taking her money. It would have been in 1961, near Christmas time. Neil came back for the holidays and found out. But there was nothing we could do. I was still at school and mam said Neil had to finish college, so she'd stick it out till then."

"She wouldn't just leave him?"

"Get on! Where would she go? Anyway, this went on for two and a half years. But when he left Liverpool Poly, Neil had an offer to go teach in Australia and she went with him. Then a month later, our dad was dead. Walked in front of old Fred Lakin's lorry they said."

"And all that time he had been preaching at this church?"

"Oh, yes!" Marian put in. "And the funny thing was, at first people came to listen to him. Do you mind how imposing he was, so tall and skinny, always wearing black? He looked like a mad preacher, and he was one. You should have heard him. Some folk seemed to like his ways – all this 'I've sinned terribly, and you have sinned terribly," – it went down right well, for a spell. But then folk must have seen how mad he was, mad as a hatter. And sometimes he used such bad language. In the end, there was no one. Just as well he died, if you ask me, no loss there."

"And all this sin, John, was it remorse for how he treated you and your mother?"

"No, if anything he beat us worse then. No, his "sin" was all in his head. Come from reading the Bible too much, I think. No, really, he was just plain nuts I reckon, and we were all too scared to see it."

Marian was bored with talk of the old man. "Anyway, that's enough about him. Tell me about yourself and living in America. Fred says you're a stockbroker, so you must make lots of money. But he also says you're a writer. Which is it? D'ye have one of those big Cadillacs?"

"Sorry. The stock market is just like any other business, it has its ups and downs. Right now, it's all rather shaky. I drive a BMW, though, just a little one. And I'm not really a writer. But I might try. I've written some technical stuff already, but that doesn't count."

"Get on," said John. "You was always the clever one. Our Neil worked hard but he was never as clever as you was then. Are you married?"

Reluctantly, Philip told the Holyroyds the basics of his life in America, including his divorce. After all, it was only fair, a fair exchange for having pumped them and everyone else in Cottisthorpe about *their* lives. But he hated talking about himself.

"It's funny, but" John put in when Philip stopped, "you

only lived here a few years and yet it's like you know us well."

"I think it's because of which years it was. Just the right years to make an impression."

"Yet you never came back, til now."

"I know. I was miserable when my parents moved to London, and then all my friends, like Neil for instance, all left. None of them, as far as I know, came home to work after University. And I had no relatives here, no one to stay with. So coming back never really was an issue. After my father died, I had even less reason to come to England. Then this year I just had the urge to see what it was like. So here I am."

"And you want to write a story about us?"

"Well, I want to write a story, whether it will be about Cottisthorpe, I don't know. I'm just gathering what they call 'color' – ideas and situations. It'll be years before I can weave it all into a novel."

Marian asked, "And you'll give up your business?"

"Heavens no! It's nothing serious, more like trying a new hobby on weekends and vacations."

Both John and Marian Holyroyd seemed dubious about the whole idea.

"Sounds like a lot of fuss for nowt much."

"Think of it as nowt much worth a fuss, instead."

They all laughed.

"Mebbe that's right. Mebbe that's right. But nothing happens here. You'd best drop it, I reckon."

"There *is* something I wanted to ask you though, John."

Holyroyd stood up. "Some other time perhaps. I must be going now. Marian doesn't like me hanging around the pub all evening, do you, Marian?"

Now they were all standing.

"It's all right if I'm here to keep an eye on you. I hope I see you again, Philip. Before you go."

"Perhaps we could all have a drink together later this week?"

"That'd be nice. Bye."

After the Holyroyds left, Philip sat at the table for a while remembering that terrible man, the tiny little house, and the fascinating mixture of happiness and fear, created by the mother and father respectively. He knew a little of the family history. She had been the village beauty and Holyroyd (Philip couldn't recall his first name, but it was something biblical) had grown up in Cottisthorpe, son of a cobbler who was also a popular lay preacher. The father and son traveled around the villages on Sundays, preaching at tiny chapels that couldn't afford their own minister.

Elizabeth Smith, whose father had been a genuine village blacksmith, had played the organ – an old foot pedal-driven harmonium – in the Methodist chapel (he couldn't remember the name of the village, though he and Neil had visited it). The Holyroyds, father and son, came one Sunday and her parents had them in for Sunday dinner after the morning service. She fell in love with the tall, gangly young man with his earnest words and intense eyes, and the black city suit.

That would have been in 1939 or earlier. Neil's father had spent at least part of the war as a conscientious objector, driving an ambulance – ever after he had been very proud of the fact that he could drive, even though he didn't have a car. His job at Minton's had to do with repairing the machines.

Probably the violence and abuse had always been there, but the sharp turn towards even more religiosity had come in late 1961. Was it because Neil, his favorite, had left home or did it have something to do with the death of little Angela Hand? Philip could feel the idea building. He could see the old man as a child molester. A killer perhaps? No, it was too fanciful, but then *someone* in this town had killed her. That might explain why John, and Fred too perhaps, were so anxious to head him off, and why John had whisked Marian out of the bar tonight: a sobering thought.

It wasn't until he had changed for bed and was staring out over the back of the town that he realized something odd and a little sinister. He had never told John Holyroyd his story about being a writer. When and where had Holyroyd picked that up?

CHAPTER 20

The next day was Sunday, so he drove out into the country, exploring, binoculars at the ready. He got as far as Rutland Water, which he knew was a major sanctuary for wildfowl. The sun was even hotter, this day, and few birds were visible, just some rafts of gulls far out on the water. The level was down and the fabled drowned church on its little peninsula didn't look quite so drowned.

The shores of the lake were full of jolly families picnicking and Philip felt out of place. After a while he headed back to Cottisthorpe, stopping for a long time by a cricket match being played in time-honored fashion in a field by the church. A romantic ending to a hot, peaceful, English Sunday.

And all the time he thought about the two murders, although there seemed no sense in any of it. Perhaps the library would hold more secrets. Historians always go back to the written record.

It turned out, next morning, that the Cottisthorpe library had only a very small section on criminology. He scanned it quickly in the hopes of picking up something. At first, nothing seemed likely to contain useful information, most of the books being nineteenth-century reference works and mind-numbing compilations of county regulations. But on the bottom shelf he came across a work entitled, *Landmark Capital Cases of Twentieth Century England* by Jan Franklin Tower. In the index: William Edward Green, executed 1952.

The author, who evidently opposed capital punishment, had done her homework. The case was spelled out exactly as he had put it together from the newspaper report, but the difference was that right from the beginning she made it clear that she had doubts about the whole thing. Halliday's interest began to rise. She wrote elliptically in places, presumably for fear of libel or something like that. But she had made it plain by the end of two pages that she thought Green had been executed for a crime he didn't commit, or at least, the prosecution had not proved the case.

All the evidence was highly circumstantial. To be sure, Green had been seen in the vicinity of the child's house that day, but he was a relative of the neighbors and was around there all the time. He had a prior record but there was no direct evidence at all linking him to the case. She wrote:

"While there is no doubting the revulsion that all society feels concerning a sexual crime against a minor, and especially one resulting in death, the speed with which the trial was brought to a conclusion hardly does credit to the severity of the charge against Green. The defense repeatedly showed that there was no evidence directly to place Green at the scene of the crime during the interval in which the police doctors concluded death had occurred. In the end, Green's lack of a credible account of his exact whereabouts on the afternoon of December 5th, 1951, seems to have weighed heavily with the jury of 12 men who took but 35 minutes to reach their verdict.

"In the Court of Appeal, Mr. Justice Applewhite similarly took only a brief time to conclude that there were no grounds on which to overturn the verdict. No further appeal was attempted, and Green was executed a mere three months after being found guilty, his death representing the last execution at Leicester Gaol."

Philip sat and wondered what might lie behind these cool, firm statements, so formal in contrast to the fury of the newspaper diatribes against Green. He could understand a rush to convict, but in Britain, surely, or anywhere in the world, the presumption of innocence was paramount. Could it really have been the case that there was no direct evidence linking Green to the murder? On the other hand, the prior convictions for molesting a child, plus the lack of an alibi, had been enough. Nonetheless, he was surprised – he had expected any account of the trial to show an airtight case. He had assumed that the police would have had a stronger case than that.

Ms. Tower's book had been written in 1978. None of

the other books in the library mentioned the Green case. He wandered out into the sunshine half-lost in thought. Even so, he noticed the woman sitting in the reading room who got up after he passed and followed him out. A very attractive woman, dressed in a dark skirt and a pale green blouse.

He strolled down the marketplace wondering where he had seen her before but couldn't decide. With his stomach growling, even after one of Queenie's massive breakfasts, he went off to find a cup of coffee and some biscuits in the small knot of shops built where an old furniture store used to be. As he stood in line, he glanced in the adjacent store window – a bookstore – catching in the glass a reflection of that same dark-haired woman, now looking at him from the street entrance. Then he remembered. Bursting with curiosity, he bought the coffee and walked further into the little alleyway of shops instead of sitting down to drink it there. Then he quickly turned and walked back.

The dark-haired woman immediately sat down at one of the tables, with her back to him.

Feeling rather daring, but quite confident, he walked around and sat down opposite her. The way she failed to look up, but sat quite still with her eyes down, almost resigned, showed him that he was right.

"I thought I should say "hello.'"

For a long time, she sat motionless, so long that he wondered whether she was ill – she sat so silent and unmoving. Then she raised her face towards him. All he saw at first was her eyes, so dark they were almost black, and impossible to read.

"I'm not very good at this, am I?"

She had just a shade of the local accent, otherwise it was straight BBC.

"I don't know. If you've been following me ever since New York you're great." He tried to smile.

She raised her eyebrows in surprise as he spoke – he noticed that they were thick and dark chestnut-brown like her hair. Had she not known he was American?

"It was just today and – well – the other morning. But I thought...they said... oh dear, let me start again. I thought you were English – local in fact, from..."

"I am, or rather, was. But I've lived in the States for the last 20-odd years, so I guess I am more American than not. I guess I sound American."

"I guess!" She smiled faintly.

"Alright. I suppose."

She smiled again and then caught herself. She looked down at the table.

"Why are you so interested in that murder?"

"Why are you?"

She looked up again, now frowning, speaking fast.

"She was my sister... she was my little sister. She's nothing to do with you. Why are you so interested? Couldn't you just leave us alone?"

He felt flat and confused. What should he say? Which one was her sister? The Cottisthorpe child, presumably. What was going on?

"What can I say? I'm terribly sorry – about your sister, I mean – you know, I wasn't so very interested at first. I barely remembered that there had been a murder. Then I was just reading through old newspapers and saw the reports, which made me realize that ever since I came to town, everyone has wanted me, in the worst way, *not* to be interested. And now I'm being followed. Let's see, you must know John Holyroyd, that would explain it. Did he tell you to follow me? What is this – an Agatha Christie novel and you're Miss Marples?"

Stung, she looked up angrily.

"She was my sister!"

"I know, but then what? What's special about all this? Oh look, I don't mean it that way. Of course it's special and terrible, to you and to everyone. I mean now. Why are people so especially keen that I should not be interested in this? It was over 25 years ago."

"Twenty-seven, And still unsolved."

"Can we start from the beginning? I'm Philip Halliday. I live in Philadelphia. I went to school here in Cottisthorpe from 1954 to 1961. Then my parents moved to London. Until this week I hadn't been in Cottisthorpe since then.

"I'm a stockbroker. Nothing more sinister than that. I decided to take a holiday here for a few days and got a very vague idea of writing something about Cottisthorpe in the old days. You have to write about something you know, you see. I loved it here in the fifties. Everywhere else we lived was just for a year or so at a time. I felt roots here, except we left anyway. Then I went off to university –

Durham – and then to America. This is the first time I have been back in all those years. But it is the only place in England that I really know as home.

"I came, looked around, read the old papers, and I might have already left. But I became very curious simply because people didn't want me to ask questions. Now I have a mysterious woman following me. Your turn."

"My name is Jean Hand...."

He sighed with relief; at least he knew what they were talking about.

".... I'm a teacher, and headmistress of Oakways Primary School. It's new, you wouldn't know it, I suppose – on an estate out along the far part of the Three Oaks Road. I've lived in Cottisthorpe all my life, except of course for university – Oxford – and five years teaching in Somerset. I came back in 1971. John Holyroyd told me that you were poking into things – about my little sister, I mean. He asked me to follow you and see what you were up to. I'm sorry!"

They both fell silent.

"It's odd," he said finally. "I knew almost nothing about your sister's death until a few days ago. It happened after I left, when I was a first year in university, I didn't take much notice of the news. It was in all the papers. Of course."

She said nothing.

"Do you know that the microfiche films for that year's newspapers are missing from the library?"

"Yes, I know they are, but I don't know why. Is that why you went to Nottingham, to go to the library?"

"Yes. Actually, I read about it first here in town anyway. The 1962 papers ran a story on the anniversary of the killing – 'why haven't the police acted,' that sort of thing."

"Of course."

She seemed distant and inevitably he thought, "She took those films – and she goofed." He decided to probe.

"Silly really."

"What is?"

"Well, there is a complete set of films in Leicester and no doubt the London libraries, plus all the national papers on file."

"I don't know what you mean."

"If someone wanted to discourage nosey people, like me – by lifting the microfiches. Not very effective."

She moved awkwardly in her seat.

"Why would anyone want to do that?"

"Oh, come on! Why would anyone follow me?"

Suddenly she flared out.

"We don't want outsiders interfering in our business!"

"Suppose an outsider finds out who killed her."

He wasn't sure why he had said that – it really didn't make any sense – until he saw that was exactly what he was trying to do. He was playing the detective. After all, it was an engrossing puzzle. So she was right, in a way; he was interfering.

But now she surprised him again.

"Do you think anyone could? After all these years?"

She wasn't dismissing the idea; she was considering it.

"Well, probably not. I'm not a policeman. If the police didn't solve it then, surely no one can now."

"Are you trying, though? Isn't that what you're doing?"

"Honestly, I don't know what I'm doing."

"Then leave us alone!"

"I know. Everyone wants me to go away."

"I don't think they want to chase you away, but the police *are* somehow on the defensive about this – they didn't find the killer, after all. And we are all getting that way...."

"... because he or she is still around, perhaps still in town, someone you know, a neighbor, whatever?"

"Yes. It means no one can really forget, put it behind them. Even though it was 27 years ago. You know, no matter how hard I try I really can scarcely remember her."

"The killer might be dead long ago."

"Yes, but that doesn't help much. It's the not knowing, you see, that has power. Power over us all."

"Ghosts." Instantly he wished he had said something less trite.

"Worse than that in a way. All sorts of fears – in a way, including fear of finding out who did it."

"And the films are missing."

"Which makes the fears real."

"And evidently some people don't want to know the answer. They want people like me to be discouraged."

"I thought I felt that way. But now I'm not so sure."

"And Holyroyd?"

"John wants to know who did it. The pride of the

police is at stake, even though he was barely a teenager then. But on top of that, he's trying to protect me. So that's why he's being so peculiar to you. Sorry."

"It is a small town."

"Very."

There seemed nothing more to say. But the conversation couldn't end there. So he asked if she had eaten and they both discovered that they had only had coffee since breakfast. He looked at her and suggested salads. To his surprise, after a distinct hesitation, she agreed.

He got up and waited in line for two small salads, crusty rolls and a cheese plate. She wanted hot tea, and he had a lemonade.

As they ate, he studied her. He decided she must be several years younger than him. She had just a trace of frown lines and a few laugh lines at her eyes. There was something compelling about her now that she had relaxed. She was lovely, or at least very attractive, but apparently quite unconscious of it. Her face was an almost perfect oval, with large eyes for the size of her face and a rather small mouth. A very assured face. Her hair was cut to end evenly at her collar with just a little wave. He thought it might be dyed – the color was so beautifully dark with chestnut highlights. But then she must have dyed her eyebrows too – did women do that? She was very English, he decided. Her clothes were "sensible." No doubt if he could see them under the table, she was wearing sensible shoes. An individual in a career where conformity and being "capable" was expected. Beautiful, really, in a calm, serious way.

"You know, I used to hate this town," she said out of the blue.

"My mother died a year after the murder. She had terrible influenza. An acute gastroenteritis killed her. But now I wonder whether she didn't just die of a broken heart. I was packed off to live with my aunt Hattie and she put me in the catholic boarding school – you know, Sant Elizabeth's convent here in town. Luckily, I only had two years to go. When one of her children left home that made room for me, so I stayed on at the convent as a daygirl. After university, I didn't want to come back, not anywhere near this town. But my stepfather was getting to be a problem – sick and lost his job. So I came back just to keep an eye on him.

"You don't like your stepfather."

"I didn't say that."

"Your voice did, and you sort of ducked your head when you mentioned him.

She looked down at the table where she was systematically crushing her paper napkin into a ball.

"You notice too much."

They went back to their salads in silence. Philip enjoyed the slab of local pork pie and strong Coleman's mustard. The cheese was particularly good, dry and sharp, a perfectly aged cheddar.

"You know, this is very nice."

"The cheese?" She looked up puzzled as he blushed.

"Well, that is, I was just thinking how nice it is, sitting here having lunch with you. It was a silly thing to say, forget it. I guess I'm used to eating alone. Sorry."

She said nothing but continued eating.

Philip tried to eat, but he was caught in the strangest feeling. All of a sudden, he wanted to reach over and touch her. She was so pale, so calm. He wanted to hold her in his arms, to feel that thick hair against his cheek, feel the rough tweed of her skirt against his hands. He could sense the warm softness of her cheek. This was crazy. He had only spoken to her for 20 minutes. What was happening to him? He ground one foot into the other until the pain built up.

"Is there anything the matter?"

"No, I'm fine. Just got a bit too much of that mustard."

He was perspiring; that explanation might do.

She smiled, an odd almost wry smile.

"I've heard about American mustard – like flavored salad dressing, isn't it? This is the real stuff."

He remembered that "salad dressing" was their term for mayonnaise. The crazy mood started to pass, and he was back in control, although he found himself focusing on the way a few loose hairs curled up and around her ears, the tiny gold earrings, her small, square hands.

They talked about foods, local specialties like pork pies and various game pies, and local restaurants she recommended. She mentioned a place in Sileby (about 20 miles away) in an old schoolhouse where the cheeses were perfect.

"Perhaps we might go one night."

Again, the wry smile, "maybe."

He dared not follow up, not right away, being sure she would put him off. So they talked some more: of things American this time, all the pizza, hamburger and other fast food places that had invaded Britain in the last 20 years. And Indian, he pointed out, somewhat in defense.

"Yes. I'm so used to them I no longer think of them as foreign. And half my children are Asian."

He stared.

"I'm a schoolteacher, remember? One of the parents runs a super place just along the High Street, a little way past your hotel and on the other side. Do you like Indian food?"

"I love it, and it is not at all common in the States."

"I'll take you there sometime," she said suddenly and then looked quickly down at the table.

Philip tried to respond in a cool, measured way but wondered if she saw his eagerness.

"All right, I'd like that."

Not much later they parted, after she insisted on repaying him for exactly half of the bill.

"Can I see you again?"

"Well, yes..."

"Tonight?" He amazed himself.

"I have to go to a meeting, the RSPB. Very dull."

"I saw the notice in the paper."

"You're a bird watcher?"

"Since a boy."

"Well, it's a free country." She grinned and strode off down the street, taller than most of the other pedestrians and somehow more confident and graceful. She was quickly out of sight, so, having nothing better to do, he went back to the library – smiling to himself with pleasure.

Back to the library. He took down *Landmark Capital Cases of Twentieth Century England* again and made a note of the author's name. Then he went back over to "reference" and looked her up in *Who's Who*. There she was, Jane Franklin Tower, retired lecturer in law at University College London (never a comma between College and London, he recalled). He noted her address – a place he had never heard of in Hertfordshire and returned to the hotel.

On the way, he stopped at the public telephone outside the bank and called directory inquiries. After a little difficulty, he got Ms. Tower's number and called it. An elderly but firm voice answered and after only a few moments of introduction said that she would be delighted if he were to drive down the next day and see her. She carefully spelled out directions which he wrote in the back of his notebook – it looked rather complicated – and, feeling oddly jaunty, went to take a long, hot shower.

CHAPTER 21

During the walk back to the hotel, putting his thoughts in order, he was reminded again of the incident on the Leicester Road in Wigstall. Just as he crossed Victoria Street, a car engine revved very loudly behind him. Philip jumped and looked around. It was only a young man in an ancient Land Rover, parked by the curb and revving noisily while two girls climbed in, giggling. He stood motionless for a moment.

He knew he had been putting off this thought: it had not been an accident. Cars do not accidentally bounce over the curb onto the sidewalk ("pavement" in England), not very often anyway. Perhaps it had been just some old driver not paying attention. But perhaps not. The timing was too suspicious, except that no one could possibly have known he would go to that allotment. He hadn't known himself. Unless they had followed him. All of a sudden, he felt a little scared. The woman in the blue car, farther down the road; she had been watching. Had that been Jean?

The Royal Society for the Protection of Birds is one of Britain's most popular and successful membership organizations, with chapters in almost every town. The Loughborough group evidently held some of their meetings in the surrounding small towns and villages. Tonight's meeting, he knew from the paper, was to hear a talk with slides on the birds of Nepal. He had half thought about going anyway but had thought he would be too shy to walk in on a group of strangers.

The meeting was in the new addition to the library. A small meeting room beyond the children's room was decorated in rather too bright yellow paint with Formica tables and uncomfortable stacking plastic chairs. About 20 people had assembled. He got there a little late, not wanting to hang around looking out of place. Jean, sitting near the front and dressed as she had been at lunch, looked back and smiled at him. He felt an absurd glow.

The talk was quite good and was followed by discussion and then tea and cookies (biscuits, here). Before the tea was served, however, those present were encouraged to talk about birds of local interest. Philip nearly asked about a place to see kingfishers but decided not to draw attention to himself. He could ask Jean privately. Someone had seen a pair of nesting barn owls. Another reported on a red kite they had seen in Wales. Several boasted about the trips they would be taking later in the summer. It was all a very pleasant birder's evening, and he started to enjoy himself, even when a short, middle-aged woman put up a slide and asked if anyone knew what the bird was. She had taken the picture in Virginia.

The evening speaker ventured that it was a gray-cheeked thrush, pointing to the large spots on the brownish breast. Philip squirmed in his seat but said nothing.

After the more organized part of the meeting ended, the guest speaker was promptly taken in tow by a very well-dressed woman, very sure of herself, Philip thought. Judging by the noise level, the refreshment period was an important ritual. He decided to take a cup of tea, just to see if he could get a chance to talk to Jean, who seemed to have two teenage boys with her. Just as he managed to edge close to her, however, he was distracted by the secretary of the club who wanted to introduce himself and find out who this stranger was. A rather nice man who worked for the County government, he seemed extremely knowledgeable about British birds. He was just asking what Philip's opinion of the Virginia "thrush" had been when Jean caught Philip's eye and with a rather wicked grin and grabbed the woman with the "thrush" picture, pushing her forward.

"Mrs. Mason, Philip Halliday is visiting from America, he can tell you what that bird is."

He watched Jean slide off to another part of the room while he was stuck with Mrs. Mason and an attentive Mr. Evans.

"What did you think of it then? It wasn't a thrush was it."

"Well, it depends on what you mean by a thrush, Mrs. Mason. It had a pale bib and dark markings on the cheek. If you took the picture in the late summer or early fall – er, that is, autumn – it was possibly a juvenile robin. An American robin, of course. You must have seen lots of the adults – a rather course bird compared to a real English robin."

"Oooh, you are smart. It was in September. Last year. A robin – I'll go look it up."

"Well, as you know, they are all thrushes anyway."

"I suppose they are. But fancy you being here and knowing my bird. Come on, let's tell Jean."

Not unwillingly, he was not dragged across the room to be presented in triumph to Jean, who seemed to be trying not to laugh.

"There, what did I tell you. Knows everything, Mr. Halliday does... about birds, anyway."

Philip didn't know how to take all this. Before he could say anything, Jean was monopolized by someone else. Abandoned and feeling sour, he turned to find a place to put his cup down and made for the door. She was just making fun of him, making him feel out of place. Punishing him, perhaps, for coming to the meeting. Anyway, he couldn't just stand around like a miserable love-sick schoolboy. Then he felt a hand on his arm – knew it was her.

"Sorry, this is a bit of a crowd. Would you like to go to that Indian restaurant I told you about? Tomorrow?"

"I'd love to."

"I'll meet you at the hotel then. About six, in the bar. Goodnight."

Surprised and pleased, he strode off through a market square that was oddly busy. At first, he couldn't account for the large crowd this late at night – well, a quarter to ten. But it was the Bingo Hall emptying, formerly the cinema. A second group emerged just as he was passing, and he had to jostle his way through. Then he heard a voice, right by his ear.

"Fuck off, Yank!"

Before he could turn, a foot stamped painfully on the back of his heel, wrenching off his shoe. Instinctively he looked down, and when he had retrieved his shoe there was no one in view who might fit the voice.

CHAPTER 22

Philip was up early and finished his breakfast – larger every day. This time he had the ham as well as the eggs – and was on the road before 8:00. Any thoughts of packing up and going back to America were forgotten. This was now a personal challenge. The incident outside the bingo hall had settled it. He'd be damned if these damned Brits were going to run him out of town. They had helped open this Pandora's box, and he was going to follow the story to the end. And in any case, until he resolved all these bits of unfinished business, he would never know where things stood with Jean.

Everything else (dreams, stock market, senior partners) forgotten, he determined to play detective in earnest and maybe he would write a book out of it all. And even give up the business. On this cloudy morning, flying down the MI motorway, he was feeling great about Jean, mad about whoever was trying to get in his way, and generally the world was his oyster.

The further south he drove, the more he wished he had taken side roads. Trucks (lorries) although small-sized by American standards, dominated the road. Not by aggressively cruising the middle and outer lanes, practically coming to a stop on the steeper inclines, but by constantly pulling out and crawling around each other, blocking the road. The fast lane was another sort of hazard – cars driven at 80 mph or more, lights flashing to clear you out of the way as if this were an autobahn. Not for the first time, he wondered if all Brits in cars had a death wish – it was where all of their frustrations at no longer being Top Country came out.

To hell with it, he pulled into the fast lane too and ran with the maniacs at 85.

But at least the roads were superbly sign-posted, and it was easy to find his way to Colney Heath, just outside St Albans, where Miss (he recalled the emphasis on Miss) Tower lived. It turned out not to be some cheery thatched cottage peeping over a hedge filled with roses, but one of a modern development of look-alike bungalows with neat gravel front yards. They were so similar that it wasn't easy to see which driveway matched up with which house.

Miss Tower had been watching for him. She opened the door so quickly after he knocked, she must have been standing there, waiting for him to drive up.

Janet Franklin Tower turned out to be a small, thin, busy, and almost fierce woman. She offered him "morning coffee," affecting an air of great surprise that anyone would be so determined as to drive all the way down from Leicestershire so soon. "Oh, you came," she seemed to want to say but was too polite. Really, she was eager to talk.

As they sat in a brightly lit parlor, she lectured him from the file in front of her. Evidently deciding that he was respectable, even though he had an American accent, she warmed to her task.

It was all an outrage; that was the main conclusion she wanted to draw. It had been one of the worst miscarriages of justice this century. Absolutely no presumption of innocence. Green was guilty even before the trial started. All the evidence was circumstantial and the appeals court....

After a decent interval, he interrupted.

"Were there any other suspects?

"A good question, young man. Apparently, there were not. In these cases, the police rarely look beyond the immediate family and neighbors and lists of known problem characters. And strangers always stand out in a neighborhood like that. Or this village here, for that matter. At least ten people already know that we are sitting having coffee, at this very moment. I saw the lace curtains twitching.

"The whole family was rotten. The child's father with convictions for theft from lorries, and suspicion of robbery with violence. Mother shoplifting, one arrest for street walking before she married. None of that was in the court records. Green's accuser was the father."

"The newspapers didn't say much about the family."

"No? Well, I think you're right. The papers make a meal of these things, and they usually concentrate on the image of the innocent little child and the terrified community; leave the poor parents alone.

"The father couldn't have been a suspect; he had a cast iron alibi – at work with dozens of witnesses. But there were cousins, uncles, family hangers-on – a nest of youngish men, none of them too honest or reliable. They all moved out of central Leicester after the war. This Green hung around with them."

"So the family knew him."

"Of course. He was a neighbor, or rather I think he had family who were neighbors. He would never have been arrested otherwise – and of course, the critical point was that he had a juvenile conviction for molesting a child. Lots of children in that community you see. Young families. Hysteria. It may very well be that Green was, as you say in America, the fall guy. At least, they were only too happy to have it solved quickly. And it took everyone's eyes off them all. Meanwhile, he denied it to the end."

"You mean you think they set him up; the community?"

"Possibly. He was probably a bit simple, anyway."

"But that doesn't mean they thought he did it, is that what you're saying?"

"What I'm saying is, everyone wanted a quick arrest. If he was a bit simple, unpopular and had a prior arrest, they persuaded themselves he had done it and that was all the police needed."

"But at least one person knew he hadn't done it."

"Now don't get me wrong, young man. I'm not making a case for Green's innocence. I'm interested in the process of the law, its fairness and correctness. Our laws – yours too – depend on that. That is what separates us from those barbarians on the other side of the channel. No presumption of innocence there. Once the system has you in, you have to run for your life -- it's basically your responsibility to prove you didn't do it. I can't say. My point is simply that it was never properly proven."

Remembering the man at the allotment, he asked if she had any names of the family and neighbors.

"I probably can't help you there, young man; my interest was the trial. But let's see what is here."

She read off a few names: "Wilson, Groom, Towles…I know there were more."

"Towles, are you sure? That's a Cottisthorpe name."

"Yes. Where was it? Here. Janet Towles, sister to the child's mother. Her maiden name was the same – Towles. Why do you ask?"

Her sharp eyes fixed on him.

"Come on, young man. It's time to tell me what you know. And why you are asking all these questions. You've got something up your sleeve!"

Philip described, in barest terms, what he knew of the murder of Angela Hand and then sat back and waited.

"Well, well! How terrible! I certainly missed that. And you've obviously concluded that this murder in

Cottisthorpe is too similar to the one for which Green was executed for mere coincidence."

"Not a happy thought, is it Miss Tower?"

"Happy has nothing to do with it, young man. Obviously either yours is a copycat crime, as they say, or the same person did them both. And that would not be impossible since we are unsure that Green was the first killer. They hanged the wrong man – is that what you are trying to say, and then, even worse, left the real killer to kill again?"

"Yes, simple as that."

"Then someone has got away with two murders, perhaps even more that no one knows about. There must be a way, I suppose, of checking on other murders of young girls. Did he kill again, do you think?"

"I've no idea. I haven't been through the papers after 1962. But I have a feeling there haven't been anymore, not like these two at least."

"If there had, the police anywhere in the country would have found the resemblances, long before this."

"That's what bothers me, Miss Tower. Surely the police in 1961 saw the resemblances, anyway."

"Perhaps, but then you may be giving them too much credit. You see, to them the first one was a closed case. Guilty man executed, and so on. So they would have started off thinking this one of yours was a new case, and probably never looked back."

"Never, in all these years? We have. It was my first thought. And the newspaper noted the similarities."

"I'd be surprised. Hindsight helps. Nowadays it would have been a – what do they say – a doddle to link the crimes. But in those days, they didn't have fancy computers or any of the modern forensic techniques, DNA for the semen and so on. And the molesting and killing of children is not uncommon, in this unhappy land. They will have treated it as a unique case. And, of course, it would have been a different set of detectives investigating. They always look for people with a record of similar crimes, but Green's name wouldn't have been there. And think, I researched Green's case without finding anything."

Philip went back to probing about the first murder, hoping that Miss Tower's files would hold something to link it to the second. But there was nothing more she could add. Turning down her offer of lunch, Philip headed back for Cottisthorpe. Mostly he wanted to drive slowly along by himself because some of this was beginning to fall into place.

He was back in town by 3:00 pm, having stopped for a sandwich in a surprisingly attractive motorway restaurant. It was yet another glorious afternoon, so on impulse he drove to Jean's house, finding it fairly easily. But she was not there. He headed into town and then on through. If he was going to think, the best place would be by the river.

He parked at the mill and walked up to the weir. The sun was really hot here out of the breeze, and he lay back against the grassy bank, deep in thought, until about 5:00, when he got up and went back to the hotel to change, unsure about what to wear.

CHAPTER 23

At a few minutes before six, he went down to the bar, rather formal in a blazer and dark blue shirt with no tie. He knew it made him look rather American, but that was all right. He couldn't pretend to be someone he wasn't.

Fred Lakin looked up and waved as he came in. The old man, Wiggy, was at the far end of the bar, again with a half-pint glass. He looked over and then quickly put his head down.

"What'll it be?"

"Nothing, thanks Fred. Maybe later, I'm on my way out."

Just then, very prompt, Jean walked in. She smiled at Philip and seemed to start to nod towards Fred when her face fell. With a scowl, she turned towards the door.

"Let's go then, no point in hanging around."

Philip followed her, looking back around the room. There was no one he recognized there, just a couple of people at a table, plus Fred and Wiggy. Something had upset her. It hadn't been Fred, so it must have been Wiggy.

As he followed her out to the street, he could tell from the stiff way she walked that she was still upset. He caught up with her and they walked side by side for a while.

"Is something the matter?"

She didn't break stride, but he could sense her start to relax.

"No, it was just that old man in the bar."

"The one they call Wiggy?"

"You've met him then?"

"Not really, he's been there a couple of evenings and Fred said something to him."

"Yes, Fred gives him beer. Which makes him worse. Terrible old drunkard."

"I'm sorry, Jean. Can we start again?"

"What do you mean?"

He took her arm and pulled her to a stop.

"Good evening, Jean Hand. I'm really glad to see you. Shall we go and try that Indian restaurant?"

She stared at him for a second and then laughed.

"I'm sorry, I never let strangers pick me up. I'm going off to eat with my friend Philip Halliday."

He started to say something else, but she interrupted.

"Actually, we'd be better off inside eating than talking outside playing comedians. We're here."

"Here" was a shop whose window had been covered with a dark red curtain. A discrete sign above the window read "Tandoori Palace." She led the way in.

It really was a converted shop, long and narrow, with just one row of tables, most seating four or six and a few for two. Most of the tables were already occupied but she had made a reservation, so they sat in the window next to the great red curtain. The smell of Indian food was delicious.

Their knees touched briefly under the tiny table. He looked up, but she seemed very quiet and withdrawn. She had pulled her hair into a short ponytail, bound up with a dark red, silk scarf that emphasized the pallor of her face, perhaps also because she was wearing no make-up except for lipstick and eyeliner. She looked somehow younger and prettier and yet severe at the same time, an effect heightened by the white blouse and dark blue skirt. She had put the inevitable raincoat over the back of the chair.

When the waiter brought their drinks – dry sherry for her, whiskey and soda for him, together with a small plate of spicy hor d'oeuvres – he raised his glass.

"Cheers."

"Yes. Cheers! You look very American this evening. It's the dark shirt, I think. And Englishmen never do up the top button if they aren't wearing a tie."

"At least I'm not wearing a black shirt with a white silk tie."

She smiled.

"You look nice. I like your hair like that. It makes you look very intellectual."

"How I wish..." She laughed and seemed to relax slightly. Philip realized how tense he was.

They made awkward conversation while choosing their food. This wasn't going well. They both played it safe and ordered tandoori dishes. He asked for paratha bread and raita.

"What's that?"

"Cucumber in yogurt, just in case things are hot."

"Oh, that's right. From experience, I'd say we'll need it here. That's why I recommend the tandoori chicken. A month ago, I had a 'mild' curry that practically took the enamel off my teeth."

For the first time, he saw her laugh properly. Her dark eyes lit up and she was quite enchanting.

They ate almost in silence, except to comment on this or that aspect of the food, which was superb. She ordered Kheer for dessert ("It's the only one I know") and he had it too. As she dipped carefully into the rose-water flavored rice, he knew he was falling in love with her. It was the strangest feeling, exciting and fearful. Mostly he wanted to hold her in his arms. But he couldn't. They had only just met. But he knew.

She looked across at him carefully.

"What have you decided to do?"

"I'm not sure I know what you mean."

"You've changed since lunch yesterday. You look different, more decisive, as if you've found what you're looking for. Have you?"

She was very sober and attentive. Well, he had. She was what he had been looking for. But she didn't mean that. Did he really look different?

"That's curious, I am not sure I have, but some things are starting to fall into place. One thing I know is that someone is trying very hard to get rid of me. The other day, when I went to Leicester, someone tried to run me down."

She put her hand to her mouth, very pale, staring at him across the table.

"Someone wants to scare me off. So that means there is still something to be known if I can find it. If I want to find it."

She sat motionless, her eyes now huge and dark. If only he had any idea of what she was feeling...

He tried to laugh. "Of course, I've still no idea where to start."

At exactly that moment she put her hand over his and said, "Don't."

Her hand was cool and dry, while he felt his own was burning hot.

They both broke off, not wanting to interrupt each other. She let go of his hand and looked uncomfortable, not embarrassed but just uneasy.

"Listen, Jean, something's going on. Must be. Are you interested in helping?"

"Me? No. Absolutely not. I don't like any of this. It was all long ago. Leave it be. Just leave it be."

"Jean, I don't mean to dredge up painful memories for you – but don't you see, it's a subject that hasn't gone away. Look at John Holyroyd, it's real for him and current. He got you to follow me. And as you said, he wasn't even out of school when your sister died."

"John. He doesn't know anything."

"Then why does he keep pushing me away?"

"I told you. He's protecting me. He used to be a bit soft on me. That's all. He doesn't know anything."

After that, the evening went downhill. They made small talk. He tried valiantly to rescue the situation, but she was unresponsive. Her mouth set in a stubborn little curve which he guessed would scare her pupils, and perhaps the other teachers, stiff.

There wasn't much to lose, so he tried a different tack.

"Don't let me be a nuisance, but that man Wiggy has somehow cast a shadow over our whole evening. The moment you saw him in the bar, things changed somehow."

"Have you been talking to Wiggy?" She seemed very concerned, defensive.

"No, but he hangs around the bar at the hotel, that's all. You saw him there tonight and it put you off somehow."

"Perhaps." She shrugged, a little like a child in an argument.

"Since he has spoiled our evening, would you tell me something about him?

She started to say something, perhaps something angry. Then stopped and sighed.

"I'm sorry, I tried. This has all been very exhausting, perhaps we shouldn't have come out this evening.

Tomorrow would have been better. Somehow, it's been a very full week."

"And Wiggy...?"

"Is my stepfather. William Gregory – Wiggy. I thought you might have known."

"No, I had no idea."

"Well, he is. I know it is wicked to hate someone, but I hate him and that is all there is to it."

"But you came back to be near him."

"To keep an eye on him, keep him out of trouble. Or at least so I thought. That was years ago, before I saw how rotten he really is."

"What happened to your own father?"

"I scarcely remember him; he was one of the first British casualties of the Korean War. He died when I was only four. Both my parents grew up here in Cottisthorpe. They had been school sweethearts. When my father died, Wiggy started courting my mother. He had been a friend of my father. Wiggy got out of the Army because of some kidney problem – probably made it up. I think my mother didn't know what to do, with a child to look after, so she married him. I'm not sure why I'm telling you all this."

"Go on, though."

"Wiggy worked at Minton's then. And they had a little girl – Angela, you know about her. After she died my mother never seemed to be the same. I was too young to realize what was wrong – teenagers are always wrapped up in themselves. But she was always crying and always sick. It must have been the death of Angela. Then she got the flu that winter and it turned to bad gastroenteritis – it was horrible – and then she died.

"I was sent off to my aunt Hattie's for a while and then she put me in the convent school. I think I told you all this. It wasn't suitable, they said, for me to live alone with Wiggy. I was fifteen and just as glad. Then, sometime after my mother died, Wiggy got into a terrible accident. A hit-and-run. He was all smashed up and they didn't think he would live. But he was too mean to die. They patched him up. He had all sorts of injuries - bones and internal stuff. He had been quite a footballer in his youth, so it was particularly terrible."

"When was this?"

"Oh, 1963 or 64 sometime I suppose. Earlier perhaps, I hadn't gone up to Oxford yet. He went back to his job but eventually they fired him. He was drinking and fighting all the time. I think they felt sorry for him – he'd lost his daughter, wife and then the accident – but they couldn't put up with him. No one can, really. Ever since then, he's been living on various disability checks and hand-outs.

"I can't see why everyone is kind to him when they all hate him. He's stolen from them all, or borrowed and not returned. He's fought in the pubs and the back alleys."

"Did they find who ran him down?"

"No, just another accident on a dark night."

"Funny, though: that happened just about the same time that John Holyroyd's father was run over. Cottisthorpe was a violent place then, after all."

"No, John's dad was killed later, though I suppose it

wasn't much later. Six or eight months perhaps. I'm not sure of the details now."

She looked at him accusingly.

"None of this has anything to do with Angela's death. But I see. This is all going in your book, isn't it?"

"Well, maybe. You have to admit that it's fascinating local color."

"Color be damned, it's my life."

She sat and stared at the tablecloth. The fact that she didn't just storm off gave him hope.

All evening long he had been wanting to touch her, now he put out his hand and took hers. She didn't pull away.

"I don't care about the book. I'll probably never get around to writing anything. But I do care about.... that is, I... well...."

She interrupted. "It's none of your business."

He was silent.

"Look, we'd best be getting along." She pronounced "look" to rhyme with "you."

He stared at her, and she was startled.

"What is it?"

"You've never spoken like that before. You've always had a different accent, and just then you spoke pure Cottisthorpe."

She laughed. "By gor, our Philip, tha' looked right gobsmacked this minute. Happen you've caught me. It'll drive you crazy in the end, they say, living in two languages, like. Same as them blokes as labors in Brussels and Strasburg for yon Common Market. Go daft in the end, they all do. Reet soft in't 'ed. End up like you Yanks. Never mind, eh. Com on lad, I've yonks of work to do the morrow."

Still laughing, she got up and went to the ladies' room while he paid the bill.

"Walk me back down to the hotel, I left my car in the yard at the back." Now she was speaking BBC English again.

It was raining slightly. As they set off, she slipped her hand under his arm. It was a comfortable but slightly old-fashioned gesture. This was how he remembered couples of his father's generation, and his own parents, in fact, walking home from church. He looked down at her hair, glistening with tiny drops of rain, wishing that he dared put his arm around her. Too soon, they came to the hotel. They walked up the passage to the yard, where two young men were arguing loudly by the cars.

"It never ends, you see," she said enigmatically, as she opened the car door.

"Can I see you tomorrow?"

"No, I'm going to Derby, shopping. Maybe the next day."

She turned to go and as she did so, her hair brushed his cheek. The soft scent of her was almost unbearable.

"I wonder, Jean...look it's really quite early, would like to get a drink or a cup of coffee?"

She hesitated, automatically looking down at her wristwatch but not really reading it.

"...not here at the hotel, I mean, but surely there is somewhere else open."

"I don't...well, I suppose I can make some coffee at home."

Philip could barely believe he had heard right.

"I'll follow you in my car?"

She hesitated. "Er...yes...that would be...yes, that would be best."

They drove rather slowly in convoy up the main Coalville Road and into a maze of newer housing, eventually stopping in front of a very small two-story house, perhaps only two bedrooms, he guessed. The front garden had roses and some annuals; their colors impossible to see in the harsh street lighting. Inside, he perched on a stool in a tiny kitchen while she made coffee in the French press, neither of them saying much. Then she led the way to a small living room, pulling the curtains over a large French door and pointing to the sofa. There wasn't anywhere else to sit except two smaller and rather severe side chairs.

"I expect our houses are much smaller than yours in America."

"Yes, but then this must be a lot easier to keep warm than the barn I live in."

She sipped her coffee. Somehow the silence was warm and companionable. He couldn't tell, however, whether she was as tense as he felt. She put her cup down on the glass-topped coffee table and turned sideways to face him, starting to ask a question.

"Philip...?"

It seemed the simplest and most natural thing in the world to kiss her. For a long moment, they kissed, a teenager's chaste kiss, her lips just slightly parted and her eyes closed tight. He put his arm around her to draw her closer, his other hand on her hair, and she relaxed slightly. As he slowly stroked her back, his hand came to bare skin where her light woolen shirt had pulled up. Her skin felt warm, almost hot, and soft as silk. He moved his hand under her shirt but at once she tensed and reached to immobilize it, their lips parting. When he kissed her gently again, she brought his hand up and pressed it hard against her breast for a brief moment before abruptly pulling away.

"Philip." She said his name simply and gently, but her brow was furrowed as if she was battling with a deep, terrible problem. Then she laid her head on his shoulder and stayed there silently.

Without really thinking, he knew what to do. "Jean. You're wonderful. I think I should go now. But I want to see you again soon. I'll call you tomorrow."

She answered as if she was a long way off, speaking to a stranger. "Yes. 'Telephone' you mean. Alright. If you like, although I don't know when I'll be back from Derby." Then she sat up and looked at him, her eyes dark and pleading. "But will you drop it, all these questions about long, long ago?

"I'll tell you tomorrow, or the day after; how's that?"

"I don't suppose you're giving me a choice."

Instead of answering he stood up and held out his hands to pull her up from the sofa, hoping she would let him kiss her again. Instead, she slipped past him to the door, but he reached for her hand anyway and held it. She squeezed it tightly and allowed herself to be kissed, for an instant, at the door before she opened it.

"Good night, Philip, drive carefully."

In a glowing confusion, he drove back to the town center, getting lost once, parked in the now deserted yard, and walked around to the front door. He looked towards the bar for a moment and then went upstairs.

CHAPTER 24

Philip Jerome Kennedy Halliday closed the door of the hotel room behind him with a slight sigh. It had been a strange day, with a wonderful ending. At first, dinner had seemed to be a mistake. But Jean was... well, Jean was wonderful. He could still feel the touch of her warm, soft lips... it was like being sixteen again.

He stood for a moment in the stuffy room and wondered when he would be heading home. No question, though; he wanted to stay.

Slowly taking off his jacket, he moved over to open the window. His notebook lay on the small table where he had left it. He was just about to move it so as to make room for Mrs. Henslow's tray in the morning when he noticed that perhaps it was not quite exactly as he had left it. It seemed to have been moved and yet he couldn't be sure. Deep in thought, he prepared for bed, more than half convinced that he was being paranoid, when his bare foot touched something – something small and hard, just under the skirt of the bed. It was a cheap plastic ballpoint pen – what in England they called a "biro." Certainly not his and surely not something Mrs. Henslow would have missed in her cleaning.

Now he was sure. Someone had been there, copying his notebooks. He laughed out loud. All his "notes" about Cottisthorpe and the two murders were still in his head. In that notebook were only lists of birds he had seen, going back five years or more, and various addresses, none of them connected with this trip. Plus, as far as he could remember, only the names of Miss Henderson and John Holyroyd. How funny to think that someone in the next day or so would be feverishly trying to make sense of that.

But then... not many people had known he would be out all evening. Of course, anyone in the bar would have seen him and Jean as they left, but really the only person who had known of his plans was Jean. And it had been Jean who had looked at her watch, and, against all odds, invited him back to her house. To give the burglar more time? When they kissed, had she been rather passive because she was shy, or because her heart was not in it? No, he couldn't believe that. Not Jean. Please Lord, not Jean!

CHAPTER 25

The superb weather had broken, and it rained all day, forcing him to stay indoors when he had really wanted to go and walk in the forest over towards Loughborough. Never mind, the business of the notebook had pushed him into something he had been putting off. He ought to get all this stuff down on paper (and then keep it safe). It was getting too complicated. So all day he sat and made notes, trying in the process to get the last few days better organized in his mind – to make some sense out of it all (wishing all the time he had brought his laptop computer.) In between periods at the table, he went for short walks around the dripping town. He also made several calls to his office to check how things were going. "Very confused: was the answer, which he knew perfectly well from reading the English Financial Times every lunchtime.

He called Jean twice but there was no answer. Then at 5

o'clock, she picked up, sounding either tired or wary, or both.

"Would you like to get a meal somewhere?"

"Er, no. No, thank you, Philip."

"Could I see you tomorrow?"

"I don't know. It's all... I don't know, Philip. This isn't a good idea."

"But..."

"Telephone me later in the week. Please."

By dinner time he was deeply depressed. The whole thing made no more sense than before and the nagging fear that Jean had betrayed him was almost unbearable. But she clearly didn't want to see him again. Not able to bear the thought of another meal alone, he headed for the bar at six, wondering if John Holyroyd would be around. John might have information if he could work it out of him.

He wasn't there so Philip asked Fred for a beer with a cheese sandwich and pickled onions and sat down to wait. He was determined to find Holyroyd, and this seemed the best way to do it.

Sure enough, before Philip had finished the first of the two huge spicy onions, Holyroyd walked in. He looked around the room and came straight over to Philip signaling Fred for a beer.

"I've been looking for you." Holyroyd sat down heavily in the chair, not looking particularly friendly.

"Well, you've found me. My regular evening haunt, it seems. Anyway, I was hoping you'd be here tonight."

"Not last evening, you wasn't here then."

"That's true."

Holyroyd scowled at him, and Philip grinned and bit into the sandwich.

"Yes," he said with his mouth full, "I had a wonderful evening, Jean and I went to that Indian restaurant up the road. Great food."

He wondered how Holyroyd would react. As expected, he smoldered. The man was jealous.

"You want to leave Jean alone."

"Get lost, John. She invited me...." And as an afterthought, he added, "...as I'm sure you know."

Holyroyd's face collapsed into anxiety and confusion. Evidently, he had not known. He'd had no inkling about the previous night until someone – Fred, of course – had told him. Well, that was interesting. In that case, someone else had been in his room. But if Holyroyd hadn't been in the room, who had, and again, why? And what did that say about Jean? He felt his hopes rising again.

"You'll be leaving us soon, I expect."

It was as much as Philip could do to keep from laughing, the tone was so plaintive.

"Yes, I will. It has been a fascinating visit, but I shall have to get back to work."

Holyroyd's relief was so obvious that Philip again wanted to giggle. This large man/boy was no actor.

"John, tell me about this guy Wiggy I keep seeing around. He's Jean's stepfather, I gather."

Instantly Holyroyd was on the defensive alert again.

He stumbled over his words, but at least he was willing to talk.

"He's nowt. The town drunk, I reckon. Every town has its Wiggy, no better'n he ought to be. He lives in a cottage down by the canal. Since Jean's mother died he just fell to pieces. Worked in a garage, then odd jobs. Then he got into a bad motor accident. Hit and run, it was. Never could work again. After that, it's been a steady run of trouble --- suspected of minor offenses like receiving stolen property. Hard to catch him fair and square. Drunkenness, of course. You name it. He's all right, though."

"What was his job before?"

"Dunno. Long before my time. I suppose he worked at Minton's like everyone else."

"So he knew your father?"

"Our dad liked to think he knew everyone. But I never laid eyes on Wiggy, not as I know, till I came back as a copper. Why are you asking about him?"

"It's an interesting story, isn't it? Loses daughter, and wife. Then crippled by a hit and run. A tragedy. Do you think it was an accident?"

"Jesus, man, you're a nosey parker." Holyroyd exploded. "He were found in a ditch along the Derby Road, not far from his place. He were all busted up – ribs, back, hips, legs, skull maybe. What else could it have been?"

"I can't imagine."

John, flushed and intense, tried to change the subject.

"He's not Jean's dad, you know."

"I know. Why do they have the same name? Did she change it or did her mother?"

"How the 'ell would I know? Her real name, though, is Standish. She told me once she wished she had changed it back. Hates the old bastard, she does. Anyhow, you're asking a lot of questions. Don't. It upsets her. Leave her alone."

"Why doesn't she tell me that?"

Holyroyd got up angrily, bumping the table and spilling Philip's glass.

"Sorry. Look, just leave her alone."

Holyroyd started to leave and then came back, his face now purple and furious. He started to talk in a loud, hissing whisper.

"I know I shouldn't be sayin' this, but I might as well get it off me chest. You've always been a bloody... a bloody nuisance, you and your stuck-up airs. You was the same then as now. You nigh on killed our Neil. When you went off to live up the 'ill and was too good for the likes of us. You was Neil's only friend. Everyone in our street were like me: dumb. No one else ever went to the Grammar School, and I never wanted to. You two were pals. You could have helped our Neil, even though you was in the arts stream and 'im in the sciences. You used to do yer 'omework together, at your house. Instead, you dropped him for your new pals. And Neil had to do it all alone. But he did it, by God. He got somewhere. And no thanks to you.

"You ask questions about my dad. Well just think on.... Neil sitting at home every night trying to do homework, in that house. Mam trying to help, trying to keep everyone quiet. "Course we had no telly – too much wickedness. Then 'im spouting off all the time, yelling at us. Smackin' us all around. Talk about murders, you nigh on killed Neil. But in the end, he didn't need you or any of your fancy friends.

"Just go on home now. You're not wanted here."

After Holyroyd stormed out, Philip could only sit. Everyone in the bar looked embarrassed and Philip was too proud to leave. Then Fred brought over another beer.

"Ay oop. I saw John spill your beer. Don't you mind him, now. He's a mite clumsy, but he's a good man, you know. A good man. I couldn't help overhearing what he said about Neil. It wasn't really like that. Neil's mam decided early on that he was going to university and that was the on't. She was the one that saw him through. And he had friends too, I know. Andy Marshall, for one. When you moved to the other end of town, that was everyone's bad luck. Your'n too, for all I know.

"Thing is..." the barman leaned down to speak quietly, "...he's always been a bit soft on Jean Hand. Now I'm not saying anything that Marian doesn't know. There's never been any hanky panky, mind. Jean would never.... She's too straight, and Marian would kill 'im anyhow. But John's very protective of Jean – being an orphan an' all. We all are – and I reckon he was a bit jealous when he heard you had a meal with her last night."

"Too bad."

"Go easy, Philip Halliday. You've come here and stirred

folk up a bit. But then you'll leave and us'll have to set it right again."

"I'm not sure what you mean."

"Asking about that murder – Jean's little sister. John says it's got her properly upset. And she doesn't want to be in no book either."

"Or you."

"Me? I'd break your bloody neck." Fred was not smiling.

"It won't come to that, Fred. I promise."

But none of this was really registering. Holyroyd's words had been angry and hard, but they hit home with the bitter taste of the pure truth. And perhaps not altogether a surprise.

His parents' move to the new bungalow had coincided with the point in school at which boys were divided into "arts" and "sciences" streams. The former had almost no maths or science after that point (age about 14) and the scientists had no history or English. Everyone had modern languages, but only the arts people could keep going in Latin and Greek: a wasteful and narrow system.

But the truth, which he had never acknowledged before, was that this had not been why he and Neil had parted ways. What John had said was true. He had simply rejected Neil and his lumpish ways and moved in with the slicker up-the-hill types who had gramophones and televisions, and who holidayed in Bournemouth rather than Blackpool. He had wanted to. He preferred them.

He and Neil had been totally different. Neil's mother

had taught him to vamp popular tunes on the piano – which he did quite well. Stern Mrs. Oglethorpe, all pince-nez and metronomes, kept Philip to a strict diet of Mozart and Czerny exercises. Neil preferred soccer to rugby and hated cricket. Philip abandoned the cozy fireside at Caroline Street and tasty "high teas" of sardines on toast for central heating and dinner at 7:00.

But it was worse that than. His rejection of Neil had not simply been an accident of living in a new and different, up-scale, part of town, with different friends and values. It was deeper than that, and simpler. He had come to hate Neil.

Pausing at the top of the stairs, Philip could see Neil perfectly. Always shortish, Neil put on weight, bulking up through exercise programs he got through advertisements in the newspaper – Charles Atlas and others. He was 200 pounds (15 stones) of muscle and a bit of a bully. Many of the boys had been afraid of him. Except that he did not threaten Philip. On the contrary, he mooned about, always watching him. Wherever he went, in school or the town, Philip felt Neil's reproachful stare. He couldn't stand it and in turn went out of this way to exclude Neil, to make fun of him.

Philip couldn't stand Neil's attempts to put a gloss over his coarse accent and manners, rather like those English radio disk jockeys with their fake American accents (irony there, all right!). But particularly he had despised Neil's kicked-dog attitude. "You have everything, I have nothing. I want to be like you – to be your friend." Matters were made even worse by Philip's mother who could be exceptionally dense when it came to young people. "Why don't you invite that nice Neil over? You used to be such friends."

Philip knew he had been terribly cruel. He had been ashamed of Neil's lower-class background and hadn't wanted to be thought to associate with him. Perhaps a friendly word here or there would have gone a long way. But no, with Neil it would have been all or nothing, and "all" would have been intolerable. The more Neil tried to be his friend; the more Philip despised him.

And now, what did he think? He lay on the bed and stared at the ceiling for a long time. If John harbored such resentment, what about Neil? Had Neil long forgotten all of this, living happily in Ireland? Did Neil ever think of him? Was there any way of making up now for all of that cruelty? Suppose they met. Would he still find Neil crude and awkward? Would they both be hideously embarrassed?

All of which left the key question: was Neil the tall man in those awful dreams?

At least he could start to atone by being civil to John and Marian, if they would let him, and perhaps John would get the word to Neil that Philip was not such a terrible person after all. After that, perhaps…

He fell asleep on the bed, fully clothed, and did not dream.

CHAPTER 26

Another brilliantly sunny day in a summer without parallel, too nice to go back to the library. He decided to go to the mill. Perhaps a kingfisher would come flashing through the willows and alders like a brilliant green and blue missile. He would call Jean later, even though she had asked him not to. But he still had a lot of thinking to do. The mill would be really quiet, a much better place to think than the crowded town or that tiny room.

First, however, there was one bit of curiosity he had to satisfy. So he tried to drive to the wharf at the end of the canal, where it came into town.

He remembered the canal as ending somewhere behind a large garage that had also served as the bus station for the Midland Red Buses. But all that had disappeared. As the traffic was not conducive to idle cruising about, he pulled into the parking lot of a large "do it yourself" store to get his bearings. Seeing a narrow alley continuing down the side of the parking lot, Philip walked cautiously over and peered down it.

This was the place.

The canal here was black and smelly, decay layered on top of the familiar smell of pond water. There was no flow in this blind spur from the main canal: the water didn't circulate at all. Yesterday's rain had probably stirred it up a bit though. Bits of plastic – the ubiquitous crisp bags – floated out there, caught up on patches of green duckweed. The still surface of the canal looked as though it could be hiding waters 10 feet deep or more. Philip knew it was really only about three feet here, probably less, nonetheless the canal was somehow threatening.

Rose Wharf was a deceptive name for a terrace of drab, early nineteenth-century cottages, standing across the middy towpath from the canal. The cottages were of local brick, mellowed to an odd orange color, presenting one single face, unbroken except for doors and very small windows. Facing them on the other side of the water was a blank wall of brick, about 12 feet high, and a tall, blackened factory chimney. At the end of the row, three children were playing noisily.

Somewhere else perhaps, there would have been roses climbing the walls – "English Cottages by the Water" – but this was not a picturesque scene, just a run-down industrial landscape. A good argument for urban redevelopment. And Rose Wharf had nothing to do with roses anyway. It had been named for one Archibald Rose, a coal merchant who built the cottages for his no-doubt poorly paid wharf workers.

Having put his head around the corner from the parking lot, Philip was disinclined to venture further. It was not the place where strangers simply wandered around. He guessed there might be a yard at the back of the cottages. In fact, there must have been, because that was where the old outdoor privies would have been, and probably a space to keep a pig. If he had been more adventurous, he would have tried to find the back alley.

It was only a glimpse of Rose Wharf, a snapshot back nearly two hundred years. He stood there undecided for a moment and then retreated to the car, almost tiptoeing, not really sure why he had come. Then he drove very fast through the town and over the station bridge.

This time there were several cars in the car park of Oakley's Mill, presumably people having morning coffee or an early drink before lunch. At the weir it was not as peaceful as before. After the rains, the river was running full and fast, rushing over the weir with a steady, driving sound.

No trains ran on the embankment. Over the sound of water over stone he could hear a few birds. He automatically noted them although he had forgotten to bring the binoculars... and the notebook, damn. It was a sign of how distracted he had become. That yellow hammer must have a territory here; it was singing from the same perch in the same tree as before. There was a chaffinch and a blackbird, a reed bunting...

In any case, he had other things to think about, first sitting on the newspaper he had brought and then lying back in the deep grass still damp from yesterday's rain. Chewing on a fat grass stem, he recalled the old-fashioned mystery stories his father had loved, where the detective organized his thoughts by making lots of lists – both of evidence and suspects.

Notebook or not, the list wasn't very long. And certainly, he wouldn't need to write it down. There were only a few possibilities to test:

1. *Two murders, same person. Green executed by mistake. In that case, either the police didn't notice the resemblance between the two and just concentrated on the second case, or they saw the connections but still couldn't find the killer.*
2. *Green was the right man, then the new murder is by someone else.*
3. *If the same man did both, the way to find him was to search out the connections between cases.*
4. *If a different man did the second, it might be virtually impossible to discover who.*
5. *But it might not be literally impossible. To be sure, the murderer would have been only one of the thousands of people in this town. He might be long dead, or have moved elsewhere, in which case there was the whole country to search. Except. Except...*

> 6. *Why all these attempts to get me to stop asking questions?*
> 7. *It can only mean that someone I have met still knows something.*

So it came down to two questions. *(a) What are the connections between the two murders; and (b) who was trying to put me off. Particularly who were the people in common – between the two murders?*

It was ridiculous to think that he, a total stranger, could add anything to this pair of murders. But if that was so, people would ignore him.

Who is NOT ignoring me?

> 1. *People like Jean, Fred, John, perhaps even Wiggy and the old man at the allotment. Therefore, one of them was connected in some way to the murders.*
> 2. *Jean. She is being protected by John Holyroyd because he's sweet on her. It was her sister killed. Why else?*
> 3. *Fred Lakin. Probably also protecting Jean. But one small point of violence – his father's lorry killed John Holyroyd's father.*
> 4. *John. Protecting Jean. Also protecting his father in some way?*
> 5. *The old man at the allotment. Does he count?*
> 6. *Whoever tried to run me down. They knew I had been to the allotment and possibly also knew I had*

been to the library. (Note: what kind of cars do Jean, Fred, and John have?)

7. *Whoever bumped into me at night in the market. Unknown, could have been Wiggy.*
8. *Wiggy. The father of the second dead child. Could easily have been the one who bumped into me in the market, just out of maliciousness. But he wouldn't have killed his own daughter.*

Not a promising list. Although there was a parallel list that should be examined – a list of deaths: the two girls, Janet Hand, Amos Holyroyd, even Elizabeth Holyroyd and two hit-and-runs – Amos and Wiggy. Yes, and a possible hit-and-run attempt a week ago at the allotments.

All yesterday he had gone round and round the same questions and come up with one conclusion, only one plausible set of connections. Yesterday his analyses had all pointed in one direction and they still did: John Holyroyd's father. It was old man Holyroyd. Amos! Yes, that was his name. Amos Holyroyd was the most likely candidate: all that bottled-up violence and the abusing of his wife and sons. The tension between the Sunday bible-black holiness and the weekday sin. He had all the character traits of a killer and abuser. He could just imagine that tall black figure molesting little girls.

Amos Holyroyd knew the Hand family. He worked with Wiggy at Minton's. After the little girl was killed, he entered into a new and more violent syndrome of public religiosity. He started confessing his sins to the whole world (without actually saying what they were). When he could bear the guilt no longer, he threw himself in front of Fred's father's lorry. His wife and children had left him, and he just couldn't stand it anymore. And was that the real reason why Elizabeth left – had she guessed about the murders?

Philip sat up and stared at the opposite bank. But could Amos Holyroyd also have killed Ann Dexter? Was there actually any connection between the two cases?

Going back to Angela Hand, if John Holyroyd is pretty sure that his father did it, that's why he doesn't want me poking around. He may even feel guilty that his friendship with Jean as a boy (presuming there was one) exposed Jean's little sister to his father. Fred Lakin, too. And since Amos is dead, all this really is just stirring up trouble needlessly. And maybe the police know, too, which is why they haven't been active.

There was even a more interesting variant. Fred Lakin's father had known that Amos was the murderer. Perhaps one night Amos had actually admitted it in a fit of religious zeal. So Fred Senior decided to take the opportunity one night when he saw Amos walking the dark streets looking for sinners. And claimed it was an accident.

The man who swore at him in the market crowd must have been Wiggy. It was the sort of nasty thing he would do. And the car at the allotment. Perhaps that had been an accident. After all, he hadn't been in Cottisthorpe long enough. Even if Jean had been the woman standing by the blue car (when he mentioned it over dinner, she had seemed awkward), there had to have been a second person.

He couldn't imagine her following him and then calling in a hit squad.

It was over then. Whether Amos Holyroyd had killed both of the girls or just Angela Hand didn't make much difference. Amos was dead and that was that; except that John was trying to cover it up.

Still, there were lots of loose ends. The family of William Green would certainly be pleased if one could show that he had been innocent after all. Jean might feel better knowing that the case was at rest.

And without quite articulating it, he also knew that he wanted very badly to be able to give the solution to this case to Jean as a gift. From him.

He had just settled back in the grass when he heard someone walking over the footbridge and along the path towards him, he could hear the grasses brushing against his legs. He heard him (he assumed it was a him) come down the wooden steps by the weir. For the sake of politeness, he didn't turn around to look.

CHAPTER 27

This was a new dream – dark again but cold, very cold and suffocating. He was tied down. Someone had pinned him down and he couldn't breathe. It was dark and noisy. There was a car. He was in a car, bouncing around, going very fast. Somewhere a bell was ringing. He tried to move his head, but he couldn't. It was cold still and he couldn't breathe.

Then it was light – far too bright. Too many people were talking all around him, but he couldn't tell what they were saying. He shut his eyes tightly and that gave him a headache. No, he already had a headache. He felt that he must be in bed. It was another dream.

He waited, but the dream didn't end. Nor did it progress. He just lay there and tried to remember what the dream had been. Cold. A car, in the dark. A bell. If only all this noise would stop.

The light seemed to lessen, so he opened his eyes.

Sargent John Holyroyd was sitting by his bed. The room was quiet and cold. He was still cold. But this wasn't the hotel. The bed was a simple-looking iron frame – no, it was more complicated. Holyroyd was looking at him and speaking, but he couldn't hear at first.

"I say, Philip, can you hear me?"

Then it was obvious, this wasn't a dream.

"Yes, don't shout. Where the hell is this?"

"Well, that's better. You've been out for almost an hour. You fell in the river you know."

"Philip thought for a moment, and it started to come back. *No, I didn't. I was lying in the grass. In the sun. Someone came. Then what happened?* He said nothing.

"Someone found you in the river. You fetched up down at the mill. I'll get the nurse; I was supposed to call her directly."

Philip felt a terrible headache and a deep fear; they, both of them, reached from deep at the back of his neck to his forehead. Not throbbing, just a constant presence. He coughed and found his lungs hurt badly too.

A nurse came in, a Black woman with a thin but cheery smile that instantly relaxed him. He was happy to let her take over.

"You're awake, I see. Good, now you'll mend quickly."

"What are my injuries?"

"Nothing broken; mild concussion. Some bruising, left side of head and face, water in lungs. You must have fallen and hit your head, then the stream rolled you along a bit."

The nurse was almost reciting from a book. "Very fortunate!"

"Yes, Philip, remember all those stones by the weir!"

"How do you feel?" asked the nurse, quickly putting a thermometer into his mouth before he could answer. Holyroyd, hovering at the door, laughed.

"I'll be off then."

Philip made frantic gestures – no – stay.

"Lie still please."

He grunted until Holyroyd sat down.

"Sergeant Holyroyd. I want to make a formal statement. I did not fall. Someone hit me on the head from behind and pushed me in. I was lying down about 10 feet from the water. I did not fall."

"Who did it then?" asked Holyroyd, truculently.

"Jesus, I'd tell you if I knew. I didn't see, they came up from behind."

"You fell in."

"No. My watch is missing."

"Philip, it's probably in the river."

"What about my wallet?" He was suddenly anxious about credit cards.

"There was a wallet in with your things," chimed in Nurse Martin, helpfully. "Full of money, I had to look so as to register it properly."

"There you are."

"Go back there. Do me and yourself a favor and go back there. You'll be able to see where I was lying down.

And then where I was dragged to the water. There will be marks in that long grass."

"Well, I don't know."

"You don't know! You're a policeman! I've just made a formal statement that someone tried to kill me. Someone tried to kill me and you 'don't know?' What kind of police work is that?"

Holyroyd, very red, got up.

"I'll look in later."

"Don't bother."

The nurse watched in amazement.

"Doesn't your head hurt?"

"Yes," he said angrily. "It hurts like hell. Like someone slammed it with an iron bar."

"Well, that is what it looks like."

"Tell that to the sergeant, then!"

"Alright, now. Meanwhile, you need to rest. We won't give you any sedatives unless necessary. Concussion, you know."

CHAPTER 28

Next morning, they discharged him, Nurse Martin making dire remarks about the need to stay quiet and rest. A taxi took him to the hotel where Queenie and Doreen of course fussed over him, anxious to get the whole story direct from the victim. He went up to his room in the minuscule lift and they brought him the inevitable tray with tea. Soon there was a tap on the door. His heart leapt when he saw it was Jean, lips trembling and pale, but smiling tentatively.

She was dressed for visiting the sick, wearing a rather formal, lightweight suit, and he immediately saw it must be her church-going outfit. Not dark enough for a funeral, at least. At first, she stood far from the bed, by the window, putting some flowers down on the small table. Then she came closer and reached for his hand and her steady caring gaze seemed to tell him that his fears had been groundless.

"Oh, Philip! John Holyroyd told me last night. They wouldn't let me in to see you. Then when I just went now, they said you had been discharged. How are you? You don't look too bad."

"I'll be fine, but thanks for coming. I think it's just a little concussion and I swallowed a lot of river water. It's funny being laid up miles from home and the usual friends, though. Very lonely, actually, so you're awfully nice to come."

"I thought you might be feeling isolated. I brought you some flowers – silly, really, but I couldn't think of anything else. They're from the garden."

"No, that's great. Thanks. They're very nice. I can smell them from here, even over the taste of the river."

"You look very nice."

"Oh, thanks, this suit is a bit warm for this hot weather, though. I'll have to ask Doreen for a jug for the flowers."

Then she burst out with her questions.

"Philip, John said you thought someone had tried to kill you. But that can't be right, can it? Surely it was an accident?"

"Did he tell you that it was not an accident or just that I say it was not?"

"What, oh – the latter, I think. I don't know what John thinks. Do you really think someone tried to kill you?"

"Oh yes, I have no doubt. But the river wasn't deep enough, and he ran away before waiting to see what happened."

"No, please don't say that. Who would do such a

thing? Are you sure you didn't fall? Blackout or something? It does happen!"

"Quite sure."

"You were awfully lucky. John said the river took you down to the mill and dropped you on that little sandy area. Someone saw you from their car and pulled you out, then called 999."

"Otherwise, I might have gone to Nottingham."

"Oh, don't joke about it. It's too terrible."

"Whoever hit me must have gone back along the canal to town, not back to the car park, or he would have been seen."

"But who would want to kill you, or even hurt you?

"I don't know. Do you? Can you work it out, Jean?"

"What do you mean? Why are you angry with me?"

He daren't tell her his darkest fears.

"I'm not angry with anyone except whoever tried to kill me. Sorry."

"But you said..."

She opened her large pocketbook (handbag, he supposed) and pulled out tissues. Her nose was getting red.

"I didn't ask you to come to Cottisthorpe."

He sat back against the pillow, exhausted.

"I'm sorry, Jean. Forget it. It's just that – well – I don't know who is trying to either kill me or scare me away, or both. But I think that deep down you know it is a possibility. After all, you would prefer me to leave. So would John.

And Fred, too. They both told me to go home last night – no, the night before."

"I didn't say I wanted you to go away."

"Yes, you did. Well, okay, you said you wanted me to stop asking about your sister's murder."

Jean looked at him blankly. Almost white, except for the red-rimmed eyes and nose.

"You think it's all connected. You weren't just mugged. That your falling into the river is connected with little Angela?"

Was this an act? She seemed so naïve. Surely she had made all these connections.

"I didn't fall, Jean. And I certainly wasn't mugged; I still have my wallet."

She put her head down, starting to cry. After a moment he reached forward and held her shoulders lightly. Then she put her head on his shoulder and cried for a long time.

"Jean, hush, listen," he said eventually, speaking softly into her wonderful, dark hair. "I don't know. I have an idea about all this, but I just can't think today. But I know this: if the police go back there and find that I didn't fall, then we'll all know that somebody in Cottisthorpe has something to hide. And they're afraid I will find out what it is. I'm a bit scared, too. But unfortunately, I don't think John will go back."

She pushed herself up and blew her nose.

"If there really is someone trying to.... to scare you off, John will find him. Just leave everything to him. Please,

Philip. Look, I have to go, but please leave all this to John. He knows the town, far better than the other people in the police. They're all newcomers. John knows this town. He'll sort it out. But if you keep on like this, and if you're right about the river, then something terrible will happen."

"You can't stay?"

"No, I have to go out for lunch. I'm sorry. I'll try to come tomorrow, though."

She pushed her hands through her hair and stood up. For a moment she seemed embarrassed but before he could say anything else, she almost ran out the door.

Yes, he thought cynically. Defend John. But if I'm right about old Amos, then it was probably Good Old John who pushed me into the river. With a mate stationed downstream to drag me out just in time. But I need to know – was Jean Hand keeping me out of his way so he could search my room?

CHAPTER 29

After Jean left, Philip called John Holyroyd, or rather asked Queenie, who had appeared with a plate of biscuits, to leave a message for him.

"I was going to bring these earlier, but you had company."

She looked around the room as if expecting to find Jean hiding somewhere.

"Thanks, Mrs. ...er.... Queenie. That was Miss Hand from the school. She brought those flowers."

"Aren't they lovely?" She looked at him shrewdly. "And didn't she look lovely, too? Well, I'll go down and telephone that John Holyroyd, at the police station. And I'll bring up a vase."

Holyroyd didn't send any message back. For what was left of the morning Philip sat up in bed and thought carefully through his scenario about Amos Holyroyd.

Suddenly it was complicated again. Could he be

wrong about Amos Holyroyd? No. Amos had known the Hand family, through knowing Wiggy at work. He probably had a long history of molesting children. It went perfectly with his mad, fractured personality – abusing his family one moment and preaching a gospel of hellfire and damnation the next. Calling all the sinners to repent when he really meant himself. Somehow, he had met up with the little girl, molested her, and then killed her, just as he had the Dexter girl. Philip thought of those long, powerful hands with the clumsy knuckles and shuddered.

The problem was that left only one person who could have hit Philip over the head and rolled him into the river: John Holyroyd. He had probably worked out long ago that his father had committed the murders, perhaps even before his father had died. But he had just buried it all, as had everyone else, until Philip came rummaging into the past. He got Jean and Fred to try to discourage him and then when he guessed that Philip was getting too close to things, tried to end it.

Probably he hadn't meant to let it get this far out of hand. After all, his father was long dead. But he got worked up into a rage over "our Neil." His anger that night had been so intense, that looking back Philip wondered that Holyroyd hadn't hit him right there in the bar. Instead, perhaps he had waited for his chance. Perhaps he saw Philip's car in the parking lot at the Mill and then circled round where no one would see him, to attack from the rear.

But that didn't seem quite right. Would John Holyroyd,

who seemed such a decent, if rather unimaginative, man really have tried to kill him? In cold blood? Perhaps he had only tried to scare him. After all, he hadn't died. Perhaps he had never been in any danger of dying. But at least that would explain why Holyroyd was unwilling to check Philip's version of the story. He needed the official version to be that it was an accident; that Philip had fallen.

There were too many loose ends. Philip sat there and tried to work out how to test some of these unwieldy ideas. The first thing, obviously, was to find out if there actually had been any connection between Jean's family and the Holyroyds. Did Amos actually know them and know the child? Too bad he hadn't asked Jean just now. He got up creakily and looked at his notes. His head ached again.

The Hand family had lived on Newcastle Street, while the Holyroyds, when Philip knew them at least, lived about a mile away on Caroline School Lane. He started a list of questions to ask Jean: what church did the Hands go to? Philip knew that Elizabeth Holyroyd had insisted on taking the boys to the Methodist Chapel, while Amos Holyroyd went to the tiny Pentacostalist Church on Toll Gate. Until he started his own. Had Jean's mother known Amos Holyroyd? Indeed, when had Jean first met him?

Then there was the question of the first murder. Unless Green actually did it, could he find a connection between Amos Holyroyd and that group of people living in Wigstall? Jean wouldn't be able to help there. He would have to go back and talk to the old man in the allotment, or other people. Meanwhile, it would be interesting to see what John Holyroyd did next.

All the rest of the morning he lay impatiently in the room, waiting for Holyroyd to come. Meanwhile, he was stuck. He couldn't drive anywhere until the doctor said it was okay and that, he hoped, would be at his appointment at the clinic the next day (in the old hospital, he realized). The thought of driving gave him another question: where was his car?

When Mrs. Henslow came with a tray of lunch, he asked her to check on the car. The answer came back that Holyroyd had brought it to the hotel. Feeling foolish, Philip groped his way to the window, and there it was in the yard below. Well, he probably shouldn't drive anyway.

After lunch, he ventured outside for a slow, surprisingly shaky walk. He got as far as the park, where a few families were playing, and then went back to his room, more tired than he expected. The rest of the evening he lay on the bed going over and over the same problem. Finally, he read through all his notes and fell asleep. John Holyroyd still had not come.

CHAPTER 30

The next morning Philip felt much better. Still no word from Holyroyd. He dressed and went down to the dining room for a light breakfast – back to cereal again. After reading the newspaper, he felt full of energy and keen to get on with the day. First, however, he had to return to the clinic at the old hospital – where they kept him waiting, amid babies and ancient pensioners, until after 11:30. Nurse Martin, still with that wonderful smile, pronounced him more or less fine, but warned him to take it easy. Well, that wouldn't be a problem. After all the waiting, his energy had vanished again, and he felt only a vaguely sick depression.

Back at the hotel, there was a note from Queenie. "Please call at the Police Station and see Inspector Crow."

Philip spent too much of the rest of the day answering questions at the police station, making a statement, and then waiting for it to be typed up for signing. Inspector Crow turned out to be young – barely 30 years old – tall and earnest-looking, a schoolmaster who enjoyed authority. Also, very patronizing. He came to the point right away.

"I saw the accident report form the day before yesterday. However, Sergeant Holyroyd told me that you had made a statement to the effect that someone had hit you over the head and pushed you into the river. It was his opinion that you had fallen.

"Under the circumstances, I sent a man to the scene who found evidence that seems to corroborate your version of the incident. There were marks in the grass where you had been sitting, quite a way from the river, and then a set of marks that could have represented something being dragged to the river.

"That being the case, I called in a team of our lads who searched the area, and they quickly found a piece of wood, tossed into the weeds, with hair and traces of blood on it. The forensic office says there are no fingerprints, but we expect the hair and blood to match yours.

"I'm sorry to say, Mr. Halliday, that you have been the victim of one or more of our young hooligans. Even a quiet town like Cottisthorpe has its rougher crowd. We have had a spate of assaults like this recently."

"But my wallet wasn't taken."

"You Americans keep your wallets in your hip pockets. The ignorant local lads wouldn't have thought of looking there. That's what we use our jackets for, you know. But they did take your watch – which even Americans keep in the proper place."

"Ever since I came here, I have been mildly harassed…" Furious, Philip started to try to explain the fuller story. He told the story of the car at the allotments but saw that it was going nowhere. This man had made his mind up and there really wasn't any direct evidence linking this to the Hand murder, which after all had occurred before the Crow fellow had started kindergarten.

"Mr. Halliday. This is a town like any other, no doubt like towns in America. I've had a talk with Sergeant Holyroyd. When someone comes in and starts asking questions, folk get upset. But we don't hit other people over the head. I can't tell you what to do, Mr. Halliday. From what they tell me, you're a stockbroker, but I heard you are also a writer. Don't try to make a big story out of this. It's bad enough that someone knocked you on the head. We'll ask around and pretty soon some tearaway will be boasting of what they did, and word will get to us. It almost always does. Meanwhile, since you didn't actually see who hit you, there's no reason why you shouldn't head home to America.

Philip left, not caring if his disgust showed. On the way back to the hotel he thought briefly of trying to get in touch with Jean but decided not to. He was tired and depressed. These people were really getting him down. Later he went to the bar for a sandwich, but Fred was not there, just some young man he had never seen before. He recognized no one in the bar, so he went to bed and watched television for a while.

CHAPTER 31

What to do next? Well, he was an historian after all (or had been once upon a time). Time to go back to some basic research. The thought reminded him to call the office in Philadelphia again – how was he doing as an historian there?

He was curious how New York was responding to the fact that, after some weeks of slowly rising, the market looked unstable again. Lila reported that the head office had changed its views and was not quietly encouraging everyone to sell. Exactly opposite from what they had said before! He laughed out loud and told Lila to advise his staff to stick to their plans of buying very carefully and strategically. What he didn't say was that a New York recommendation to sell was probably the best omen of all for buying. He put down the receiver after having promised to be back soon and for a moment thought that if Lila were ever to leave, he would quit his job immediately.

Stepping out into the warm sunshine again, he heard someone calling him. Still smiling, he turned round and found John Holyroyd hurrying along behind.

"I've been all over looking for you."

"Okay."

"I've got summat to tell you."

He pulled Philip into a shop doorway.

"They went back to where you said. I was off in Sheffield for a two-day meeting. Anyway, they sent a detective. And I owe you an apology. He told me you were right. It was like one of them Boy Scout books, reading the signs. You sat against the bank, on a newspaper, there was the remains of one flying around. And drag marks between that and the river. They found a big chunk of wood with hair on it. Sorry."

"I know, I went yesterday to make a statement to your Inspector Crow. He thinks it was hooligans."

"Must have been. We've had a lot of trouble."

"So he said."

"I wanted to tell you me'self. But you sound doubtful," Holyroyd said, looking down the street away from him and talking too fast. "I know what you're thinking. But you're wrong. Your coming here has stirred up a right hornet's nest. But not this. You was lucky not to get killed, and now us'll have to sort it all out. But it's nowt to do with anything else. If you've been telling that Inspector Crow about all your questions about Jean's sister, the devil knows where it will lead. I don't mind telling you, I fear this. I'm right fearful. Only bad will come of all this – already has. The best thing for you would be to head on back to America, out of harm's way."

"John, if it was hooligans, I have nothing to fear and no reason to run away!"

"I know that. It's just... well, everything else."

"Jean, you mean. Do you think that will settle everything down, then? Everyone can go back to living the way they were?"

"You daft sod. Nothing will be the same now. You've stirred up God knows what trouble. But don't you be accusing us of trying to cover it up. We'll come to the bottom of it, never you mind. And as for someone tipping you in't river, that was them tearaways, we'll get onto them, you'll see."

"John, you're shouting."

"Aye, happen I am. Oh, 'ell, yes, I am shoutin'. But you get me that worked up."

"I tell you what John. I'll be here for another day or so, and then I really do want to leave."

CHAPTER 32

Miss Henderson, with a look of concern, came round from behind the circulation desk to greet him.

"I heard you'd had an accident. Are you alright – you look quite sound?"

"Thank you, it was nothing really and here I am back to bother you again."

"It's never a bother, do you want the newspaper files again?"

"One last time, yes, please. This time I want everything from 1964 to '75. Let's start with just the *Reporter*."

Not knowing where to begin, he searched through and found the report of the fire on Stacey Street. Frontpage headlines, the biggest event in Cottisthorpe since Queen Victoria's jubilee. He looked at the pictures of the burning buildings with more curiosity now than sense of loss, not quite able to make out number 18. Just as well.

This was silly, he had to start where he had left off

before. And there on the inside page, near the end of August 1964, he found himself staring at a picture of Amos Holyroyd. His face deeply lined, the same huge Adam's apple; the eyes mad and staring. A killer? Almost certainly.

"The death occurred last Wednesday of well-known Cottisthorpe lay preacher Amos Holyroyd as a result of injuries received in an earlier traffic accident. Mr. Holyroyd was born in 1921, the son of Cottisthorpe Methodist minister the Reverend John Holyroyd and Anne Holyroyd. A long-time worker at Minton's Cotton Mills where he was a machine repairer, Mr. Holyroyd was well known in town for his fiery lay preaching. In recent years he organized the Church of Christ's Holy Word on Nottingham Road. He is survived by his wife, Elizabeth, now living in Melbourne, Australia, and two sons; Neil, also of Melbourne, and Cadet John Holyroyd, Military Police."

He had missed the report of Amos's accident. Back one week.

"Well-known Cottisthorpe lay preacher Amos Holyroyd was seriously injured in an accident on Victoria Street last night. He was run over by a goods vehicle driven by Fred Lakin of Ashby Street. Witnesses said the streets were slippery due to the recent heavy rains. Police investigating said that no charges would be proferred. Mr. Holyroyd was admitted in grave condition to the General Hospital suffering from head wounds. Mr. Lakin is the proprietor of..."

By contrast, Elizabeth's obituary in June 1973 was very short. Presumably sent in by John.

"The death occurred last month of Elizabeth Holyroyd (nee Smith), aged 63, a long-time Cottisthorpe resident, in Melbourne, Australia where she had emigrated with her son Neil Holyroyd and his family. Mrs. Holyroyd had been active in the Methodist Chapel, both in the Ladies Guild and the choir. She was one of the founding members of the Cottisthorpe Amateur Operatic Society. She is survived by one sister, Eileen Groome of Ontario, Canada, sons Neil and John, and five grandchildren."

He hadn't known about the Operatic Society. But she did sing beautifully and play the piano – when old Amos was not there. He could imagine Amos putting a stop to all that opera nonsense.

But wait: bingo! Groome was one of the Wigstall names. So Elizabeth's sister had married someone called Groome. That might be enough to connect Amos to Wigstall. A causal visit to the relatives, the neighbor's child... Fantastic!

All morning he pored through the papers. Here was a notice of the death of Ed Clemerson, star of the Loughborough Tigers rugby team. And Fred Lakin's parents' ruby wedding. Worth looking at?

"Ruby Wedding. Lakin. Popular Cottisthorpe greengrocer, Fred Lakin, and his wife Ethel celebrated their Ruby Wedding on Saturday night with a reception at the White Horse Hotel. Among the nearly one hundred friends and relations attending were their sons Fred and

Alan of Cottisthorpe, daughter Enid from Manchester, and Mrs. Lakin's sister Elsie French of Sheffield...."

That was another of the Wigstall names – French. Fascinating; now he had almost too many names.

Just in case he had missed something, he asked Miss Henderson for the films for 1962 and 63. She looked at him curiously but brought them over. She was in a good mood today.

"You do seem to be busy this morning. Are you finding useful things?"

"Oh yes, Cottisthorpe is just fascinating. All the people and for such a quiet town, there was a lot going on in those days."

"I suppose there still is, under the surface. It's like any town, after all – 'we're not wholly bad or good'..."

He finished the quote for her:

"...'who live our lives under Milk Wood.'"

She flushed with pleasure.

"You like Dylan Thomas, then."

"One of my favorites, I was living here when the BBC did that famous televised production of "Under Milkwood." I came straight down here and read everything there was."

Now she really smiled.

"Don't let me stop you working, Eileen will make some coffee soon."

He quickly flipped through the pages until he found the report of Wiggy's accident.

"Local man in hit-and-run tragedy. Mr. William

Gregory Hand, of Newcastle Street, was seriously injured by a hit-and-run driver on the main Derby Road last Tuesday night. He was rushed to the hospital where Sister Jean Worthington said that he was 'very poorly.'"

"Mr. Hand was found in the ditch on the east side of the road at 3:00 am by Edward Towles who was cycling home from a late shift at Minton's. He told the Recorder that Mr. Hand appeared dead at first and had severe head injuries. A source close to the family said that he was not expected to live.

"This is just the latest of a series of tragedies for Mr. Hand. Two years ago, his daughter Angela was murdered in a baffling case that the police have been unable to solve. The same year his wife Janet died tragically of complications following pneumonia."

Wiggy had got the full treatment.

"William Hand, a Cottisthorpe native (damn, he wasn't from Leicester either) known to one and all as "Wiggy" has long been active in Leicestershire sporting circles. He starred for several years at centre half for the old Cottisthorpe Rovers having previously signed as a professional for the Leicester City youth team (Hell, what's this?) in 1948..."

Lots to think about here. First, he had a connection with Leicester, after all. Second, he was a young athlete. Philip started to see Wiggy in a different light – cocky, loud, sporty, glamorous to the young widow, Janet Standish, rushing her off her feet.

Just as well to check Janet Hand's obituary too; he had

read it before. It was very brief, not even giving her maiden name. Born in Cottisthorpe. Nothing there. She must have met Wiggy here in Cottisthorpe, and probably had known him all along. No connection to Wigstall. No list of survivors. Wiggy had done a poor job in sending in the information and the paper hadn't tried to flesh it out.

He combed the papers through and through but didn't find anything more useful. In the end, he hadn't found out much, but both Fred Lakin and Amos Holyroyd had possible connections to Wigstall – or at least to people there with the same surnames (family names). There was the odd fact that a Mr. Trowles – another Wigstall name – had found Wiggy lying in the ditch.

CHAPTER 33

It was time to talk to Jean about all of this, after all, so he telephoned from the library and invited her out to dinner. Surprisingly, she agreed without hesitation. They met in the hotel lobby, and she suggested that they eat at a small pub about five blocks away. The summer heat was almost stifling as they walked over. This was far hotter than anything he remembered as a boy.

From the outside, the restaurant looked to be the last place one would go to eat, just a small dingy converted pub on a corner, perhaps not having changed in the last 50 years.

"This used to be the Green Man. It was a bit ropey in your day. But like everything, it has changed. You'll be surprised."

Indeed. Inside was a cool, quiet dining room with white tablecloths and discrete lighting. A waiter in a dark suit took them to a small corner table. There was no background music, just the quiet chatter of the other diners – almost all the tables were filled.

"People come from all over to eat here. It costs a bomb, so it's bound to go bust soon. But you probably need a good beef steak to build you up. And it's always quiet, good for your headache."

They made awkward small talk while drinks came. He ordered a fruit juice in deference to his concussion, and she had dry sherry again. She wanted to know how he felt but didn't ask what he had been doing. They ordered steaks and a bottle of Valpolicella.

This place was just a tremendous surprise. The decor could happily have been from anywhere in New York or Chicago and the food was superb – the steaks cooked to perfection, the vegetables not overdone and instead of potatoes there were mashed parsnips with an orange glaze. It would have been a crime to talk during this feast, so they ate almost in silence, smiling occasionally with pleasure at the food, just as they had at the Indian restaurant. Philip found being with her like this, not needing to talk, strangely stimulating.

Then they sat back.

"I think I'll have a sweet today. I almost never do."

Philip agreed, and the dessert tray was another surprise, piled high with tempting confections. She chose fresh raspberries, and he had pecan pie.

"I had no idea there were pecans in England."

"What are they, let me taste?" She leaned over with her spoon. "They look like walnuts."

"Related, I think."

"Smashing, isn't it?"

He laughed at her use of the word "smashing," and she looked at him quizzically.

"Did you mind my taking a taste?"

"Of course not."

The waiter brought coffee and after just a sip, Jean made a face. "Not quite up to the rest of the meal, is it?"

"I'm having such a nice time; it could be arsenic for all I care."

"Not funny," she frowned.

"How long are you going to stay, Philip?"

"I'm not sure. I was going to say that I will have to be leaving soon. I've been here almost a week and I really should be heading back to the office. I've really enjoyed being here."

"Even the knock on the head?"

"Well, it was a new experience, after all."

She laughed.

"And I don't think I'll be writing a book about all this. There's probably the makings of a dozen books here, but somehow I don't want to."

"Does that make you sad?"

"I'm only sad to be leaving."

She looked down at the table.

"So this is a farewell dinner?"

"Not really."

They both stared at the table.

He started again. "Jean, I .... er ... really like you. And I want to see you again. But I feel that somehow this has been the wrong way to meet. Everything that has happened has come between us. If only we'd met some other way.... I'm saying this badly. What I'd really like to do is stop and then start all over again."

She looked up and shook her head slowly.

"But we can't do that, Philip."

He just sat and looked at her. She held his eyes.

"I think I'm falling in love with you, Jean."

He almost whispered the words and at first, he thought she had not heard. Then she smiled.

"Then stay. At least a few more days."

They held hands across the table. His heart was pounding. She hadn't rejected him. She hadn't responded directly, but her hand told him he had a chance. Finally, she let go and reached for the pocketbook (handbag) by her feet."

"I'd like to go now."

He paid the bill and they walked back through the town arm-in-arm. Before she got into her car, she kissed him quickly on the mouth and then drew back. Before she could escape, he put his arms around her and kissed her slowly and carefully—her lips, her closed eyes, her cheeks – until he felt her arms tighten round his neck and this time she kissed him fiercely back. But only for a moment before she pulled away again and half-laughed, brushing his hair back from his forehead.

"I don't know, Philip."

"Know what."

"I don't know you. Are you staying or leaving?"

"Staying. Can I see you tomorrow?" He wanted to ask her up to his room but daren't.

"Yes, please."

He kissed her again and then she pulled away as if afraid, getting quickly into the car and winding down the window.

"I think I love you, too."

He stood and watched her drive out, not noticing that the rain had started again.

Queenie might almost have been waiting for him, she darted out of the bar so quickly when he entered the front door.

"Did you get the message from Jean Hand?"

"I've just left her, she didn't say anything about a message."

"Oh, that's all right then, she just said to telephone her. About three o'clock it was."

How odd, why had she not mentioned it?

Queenie stood in front of him, bursting with curiosity.

"You two seem to be hitting it off well."

Philip knew he was starting to blush.

"Have you known Jean long, then, Queenie?"

"Lord yes, I've known her since she first went to live with her auntie, Harriet Towles."

That name again!

"And did you know Wiggy back then?"

"Everyone knew Wiggy, just like now. He was different then, handsome, a footballer – he nearly got to play on the

Leicester City team, you know. Mind you, he was always a bit of a lout, but he was handsome – all the girls were crazy about him in those days. That was before all the troubles – the little girl, then Jean's mother died, and then..."

"The hit-and-run."

"If that's what it was."

"Yes. No... wait! Queenie, what are you saying, are you hinting it wasn't an accident? Someone tried to run him down deliberately?"

"No, not that. But there was talk that some of the lads beat him up and just let it be thought it was a car or something."

"And...?"

"I expect it was nothing. Nothing came of it anyway. Just Wiggy all crippled up, lost his job – well, you've seen him. Poor Jean, she thought she'd come back to Cottisthorpe to help take care of him. When she found out what he was like, turned all mean and nasty, I reckon she wished she'd stayed away. But I must get on with the closing up. Good night, er, Philip. Take care."

That night, at first, he couldn't sleep. He lay there, still feeling the touch of her lips, the scent of her hair, her hand in his as walked along. Somehow things would all work out. He loved her. He had loved her since he sat down opposite her that first day. It was unlike anything he had felt before, a feeling that simply filled him up.

Nothing else mattered much. Amos Holyroyd was dead. Maybe the business at the river had only been hooligans, after all. And all those confusing names. It didn't matter. What mattered was Jean.

He slipped off to sleep with a silly smile on his face. But he'd had too much wine and coffee; at 2:30 he woke, needing to go to the bathroom.

"Too much coffee," he said out loud to the bathroom mirror. "And I wouldn't care if it were arsenic. Stupid thing to say."

At 5:00 am he was still staring at the ceiling. Without warning, and certainly without him knowing quite how, the whole story had fallen into place. He felt sick, destroyed. Burying his face in the pillows, he tried every possible way around the problem. No such luck. It was plain as the nose on your face – plain as pikestaff, as Neil's mother used to say. The whole visit to Cottisthorpe was turning sour, crumbling to pieces in his hands. Jean, everything. And there was no way out.

CHAPTER 34

Just as before, the row of cottages of Rose Wharf stood like a blunt reminder of the miseries of the Industrial Revolution. There was nothing romantic about their mean, squat shape even though the morning sun shone brightly on them. A breeze stirred the surface of the canal and trash circled in the lee of a wall. Little of the traffic noise from the street reached here, a backwater in every sense.

The doors and windows of all the cottages were closed, but at the end of the row two brown-skinned children, perhaps the ones he had seen before, played in the dirt with plastic toys.

As he approached, the two boys stood up. His "hello" made them move cautiously towards the front door of the last house where the older one put in his head and bellowed: "Mam!" Philip knocked on the door anyway.

A small, tidily dressed woman opened the door, obviously West Indian, with a bright red scarf around her hair. She ignored the children.

"What is it?" The terse words had just a trace of a musical lilt.

The children slid behind her, so as to watch from the safety of the room beyond. There was a smell of cooking vegetables.

"I'm sorry to bother you. I'm looking for Mr. Hand and I don't know what number it is."

All in one movement she gestured down the row, said, "Next but one," she shepherded the children out of the way, and shut the door in his face. Not once did her expression change.

The door in question was now ajar, which it certainly hadn't been earlier. Philip tapped and immediately the small, dark-complexioned man opened it. This was the first time Philip had seen Wiggy up close. His hair was bushy and dirty-gray colored, as were his eyebrows, which were set in a deep, permanent frown. Unshaven, his scarred face was severely lined, and his scowl was lopsided. He looked Philip up and down with a cold, blank stare, insolent, as if to fix his appearance for future reference. Philip saw that the blue shirt was torn at the shoulder and the corduroy breeches were held up with an old tie. He had no socks.

"Mr. Hand."

"Fuck off!"

"I'm Philip Halliday. You've seen me at the White

Horse. If you have a moment, I'd like to ask you a question."

"Fuck off, I said!"

It was the same voice as outside the Bingo Hall.

"It's about the death of Ann Dexter."

For a moment, Wiggy's face started to unfreeze as if he were about to explode. But then it went blank again.

"Fuck off!"

"How well did you know William Green?"

The door slammed in Philip's face. He stood there for a moment before turning away. How could this man be related to Jean, even by marriage?

Before he had gone more than 30 yards from the cottage, he heard a sound behind. He kept walking. There was a loud bark and simultaneously Philip felt a sharp blow to his leg and saw a quick slashing disturbance in the water ahead and heard the squawking and fluttering of pigeons.

He stumbled but didn't fall. For a second, he stood still, unable to move but determined not to run. Then instinctively he half-turned to look back.

A shotgun. Two barrels. He saw Wiggy aim again, the two barrels pointed straight at him. Nothing happened. Wiggy looked down at the gun. It had misfired.

Philip started to walk. No one called out – there was not a sound. He held his breath and walked, listening for Wiggy behind. At first, there was no pain, just a cold stiffness; but then it started to grow. He could feel the warmth of blood on his leg. He was damned if he would look back. He wouldn't even look down. If he could walk, then it couldn't be too bad. And he wouldn't run. Screw Wiggy. He would walk and not stop until he got round the corner, out of his sight. As he limped forward, there was only silence, and then finally a child crying.

At the corner of the parking lot, he stopped, leaning against the concrete wall. His right leg was starting to jerk spasmodically. He felt sick. He could see no real blood, just some red marks on his trouser leg. The pain was in the back of his thigh but his whole body throbbed. Blood was running down inside – into his shoe.

Stumbling on, slower and slower; listening for any sound from behind, he reached the street and rested a moment. He needed to catch his breath, not getting enough air. The pain was no worse, but his leg didn't seem to work properly.

He limped past the stump of the old market cross and the old-fashioned chemist's. The streets were almost empty. A few people turned to look at him, then looked away. Just another morning drunk. A little further to High Street and then halfway down would be the clinic. Got to keep moving, listening for Wiggy behind. Left, right, left. Stumbling.

Dimly he heard his name, then someone grabbed his shoulder.

"Philip, Philip!"

It was Jean, calling his name. He shook his head. Got to keep moving.

"What's wrong?"

"Leg – hospital – got to keep moving."

"Oh, God, Philip, you're bleeding. Here let me help!"

Her arm was round his waist. Both stumbling.

"You can't make it."

"Yes, we can."

He was not crying. Those were not tears on his cheeks, stinging his eyes. But Jean was crying.

"Got to keep moving, help me keep moving."

By the time they reached the clinic, she was sobbing in frustration and practically carrying him.

"Help, someone, please help us! This man is hurt!"

White coats coming. He leaned against the counter-top. Nurse Martin – blessed Nurse Martin – holding his arm.

"Mr. Halliday. What's happened?"

"Here, get a wheelchair."

"Lie down."

"It's his leg. His leg."

"Roll over, gently."

"Just pull his trousers off, quicker than cutting. Oh God, what's this?"

"Shotgun!"

"Shotgun?"

"Yes, he's right. I've seen it before. Doctor, quick. Shotgun, bleeding."

"Okay, first let's clean him up a bit. Yes, you've been shot."

"Brilliant, I noticed that!" Through clenched teeth.

"Steady now. Try to relax. You're in no danger.

Nothing major hit. I'm going to give you a local. Then we'll have a closer look. Press down here, nurse."

The pain slowly eased. He was lying on his face, sensing various pullings and probings. People were talking fast.

He lay head down on the operating table. Exhaustion filled every space in his body. He wanted to sleep.

Eventually, he was rolled onto his left side. Three nurses and a doctor peered at him.

"We've had to call the police."

"Of course, thank you."

"It's going to hurt, but it's not serious, nothing major was hit. You'll just be very sore for a while."

"I can already feel it."

"Yes. I can give you more anesthetic but I'd rather not."

"Give me another shot, I have to talk to the police."

"Alright."

Philip didn't feel the needle go into his thigh.

"I'll give you a prescription so you can sleep later."

"Thanks, later would be good. Is it alright to leave? There's something I must do."

"Well, I would prefer you to stay but I have no reason to admit you, so let's get these bloody trousers on again. Here you are. But you'll have to wait until... never mind, here they are now."

It was John Holyroyd, of course – Cottisthorpe's only active policeman, it seemed.

"Jesus Christ. You're a walking disaster area. We had a

call someone had been shot; I wasn't far away. I had no idea it would be you. But I should have guessed."

"John, where's Jean?"

"How should I know?"

"She was here, didn't she call you?"

"I just got whistled up by the station. Don't know who called it in. Look, what the hell happened, forget Jean for the moment, this is a serious matter. I need to know who shot you."

"The young lady who came in with you sir, she left." Nurse Martin – Philip was beginning to think of her as his own personal nurse – interrupted.

"John, we've got to get over there."

"What are you talking about?"

"Wiggy, her stepfather. He shot me. And she's gone over there."

"Jesus Christ, Philip, no! I told you not to interfere. Stay here!"

"Not on your life. I'm okay, let's go."

Nurse Martin called after them, but they were gone, Holyroyd commandeering a taxi outside and giving instructions, impatient while Philip, hobbling along in agony, caught up. They raced down High Street the wrong way.

"It was Wiggy, you see. Wiggy killed the little girls. Both of them. I went to see him, to see if I could get anything out of him. I worked it all out last night. He wouldn't talk to me, and then when I left, he got a gun and shot me. Mostly he shot the canal, but he got me in the back of the leg."

Holyroyd spoke rapidly into his lapel microphone again.

"How long ago?"

Philip looked at his watch. "Half an hour, perhaps longer." It seemed like days. He felt nauseous.

"Jean went with you?" Holyroyd was bitterly accusing.

"No, no! She happened to find me at the bottom of the market as I was trying to get to the clinic."

"Did you tell her who shot you?"

Philip thought, surprised. "No, I don't think I did. No."

The taxi skidded to a stop. Philip could hear a siren in the distance. Jean was standing in the middle of the path, staring down at the water.

"She worked it out!" said Holyroyd.

Two or three people had gathered outside the cottages, one was looking into Wiggy's open door.

Philip got out of the taxi and very clumsily started to limp towards her. He could feel the blood starting to flow under the bandages.

Jean looked from one to the other. Then she came to meet them, her face pure white, putting her hand out to steady Philip. She turned to Holyroyd. "He's dead. In there. He's dead... at last."

CHAPTER 35

Someone took him back to the hospital where Nurse Martin redressed the wounds and scolded him like a child. Late in the afternoon, they sent him home to the hotel.

Queenie and Doreen fussed about with hot tea and, later, hot whiskey. He lay on the bed fuzzily awake most of the rest of the evening, painfully turning one way or another, trying to find a place that didn't hurt. No-one came.

When he awoke, Queenie was sitting anxiously by his bed.

"I thought I'd keep you company. You looked so peaked when I looked in at 6:30 with the tea. You were like a dead man. And judging from what they're saying downstairs, you very nearly were. You were lucky that old sod didn't kill you, instead of himself.

"Now, don't worry yourself but Jean Hand has been

phoning and John Holyroyd asked me to tell him the moment you were fit for visitors. I wouldn't let him or that smarty-pants Inspector Crow come up last night. "Doctor's orders," I said. But John says they need you to make a statement at the station, or else they can come here if you like.

"Now, can I help you get dressed – oh don't be shy, I'd a huge husband and two boys as well as Doreen. I reckon I've helped them many a time."

"Well...."

"Oh, men! How do you think you got to bed last night?"

He saw that Queenie and God knows who else (not Jean, surely) had put him to bed in his underwear.

"Oh, er, thank you. If you could help me get vertical, this leg is stiff as a board and is throbbing like crazy."

Like characters in a comedy, they clumsily got him to an upright position so that he could limp into the bathroom. When he came out, she was still there, still anxious.

"Ooh, my! I can see that still hurts. What can I do?"

"Nothing, please. Tell Jean – Miss Hand – and John – tell them I'll be downstairs in an hour."

Pretty soon an hour sounded optimistic. It took a long time to get his undershirt off. Then it took another age to sponge down before balancing on one leg to shave.

As he looked in the mirror, he saw red eyes rimmed with black and purple shadows underneath. He stopped and laughed.

"Maroon and black. I'm the Duchess of bloody Atholl."

The worst part was putting on the trousers. Actually, getting a new pair out of the suitcase was bad. In the end, he gave up and lay on the bed, waiting. By then he had worked out that the underwear he had slept in had been clean. The bloody clothes from the day before had all disappeared. No secrets from Queenie!

Eventually, she reappeared.

"See, I knew you'd need me."

"It's just getting my trousers on."

"Oh aye, most men want help getting them off. Anyway. How were you going to manage with them shoes, and socks?"

"I know. I give up. Help me today."

"And tomorrow, most like."

She wedged him into the lift and met him again at the bottom. There also were Jean and John, the one solemn as the grave and the other beaming.

"By gor, you're up and about. It takes a lot to stop you Yanks."

"Well, we watch too many Westerns! Good morning, Jean. How are you?"

"Oh, I don't know. Better than I expected to be, yesterday. Numb, really. It's still all sinking in. But I brought you a stick in case you need it. I had to have one ages ago and they charge you a lot for these at the health service."

She held out an ordinary wooden cane, her hand trembling slightly. She did not meet his eye. There was an awkward silence.

Once again, Mrs. Henslow saved the day.

"I've told Doreen to put out coffee and toast in the bar for you. Be nice and private in there."

The bar was cool and dark, still smelling of beer and tobacco. John helped Philip ease onto a stool, sitting on one side only, and sticking his right leg out straight.

"So what happened? I was a bit woozy yesterday."

Holyroyd spoke. "He shot himself. That's about it."

"Yes." Jean leaned forward, looking straight at Philip. "As soon as you said 'shotgun,' I knew what had happened and understood why. Worked it all out. I have no idea why I didn't work it out years ago. It was obvious."

"And it was also obvious that everyone else knew," she continued bitterly, looking over at Holyroyd, "and decided to keep me in the dark."

She sat up straighter, pushing the hair back from her face.

"Perhaps that was for the best, I don't know. But I had to confront him for myself. I went into him and asked him straight out. I said, 'Did you kill Angela?' He just sat there, with this look on his face. Wouldn't answer. He didn't need to. I hit him, right across the face. But he still wouldn't answer. Then I saw that he had the gun out still, his old double-barreled, under the table. He'd had it for years. I was a bit scared, but I remembered my mother, my sister, all those years of letting him get away with things. So I just shouted,

'You're a murderer and there's no way out now.' Then I left."

"I had just closed the door behind me when there was this terrible sound and something falling, the chair going over. He'd put the gun in his mouth..." She shuddered, not crying, but deathly pale. "...He was obviously dead. Then I think I just stood there until eventually you came. John took me home."

"Nay, lass. You passed out; fainted clear away. My mates took you home in a zebra. Marian watched over you. You weren't up to much."

"I suppose so."

"Now what?" Philip was getting tired already.

"Now you two have to make statements. We got a provisional one from Jean yesterday, but she was too upset. And Queenie wouldn't let anyone near you. So... at the station, if you're up to it. There's a car outside."

"What do you want me to say?"

"How do you mean?"

"Well, shall I tell them what I think happened – the whole story – or just what actually took place yesterday."

"Just tell what happened yesterday. They can think for themselves. That's what they get paid for."

Holyroyd was probably right. But Philip had no choice but to tell Inspector Crow the whole story, at least in outline – both the murders of Ann Dexter and Angela Hand. Crow remained silently disapproving, lips pursed, the whole time. Then Philip signed his statement, unsure what would happen next.

"You'll have to stay for the inquest. Sometime next week, I imagine." Cold and unfriendly.

Before leaving, Philip asked for Jean, but she had already gone.

"There's a note for you, sir." The desk clerk volunteered.

"I've gone to start the funeral arrangements. I'll come by the hotel this afternoon. We have a lot to discuss. Thank you, Jean."

He waited for her downstairs in the empty bar, and she helped him limp around the corner to the small café where they had first met. Surrounded by curious eyes, they sipped tea cautiously. He had long since decided to tell her everything he knew, right from the beginning.

"Look Jean, I'm sorry. But this is how I see it. All this may be even more shocking to you than yesterday. But I can't hide it from you. You deserve to know, and even if I'm wrong, you need the chance to think things through and come to your own version of what happened. The only thing is.... Well.... It may spoil things for us. Nobody likes the person who brings the bad news."

"I'll kill the messenger?"

"Just as bad; send him away."

She blinked.

"Go on then. I think I know most of it."

He started right from the beginning, even telling her about his dreams.

"But that doesn't mean anything.... You were just overworked and guilty about neglecting your work, or something! Everyone has dreams!"

"I know. Anyway, I decided to come here and almost at once everyone was on the defensive. Particularly Fred at the hotel and John Holyroyd. You were a bit too, but that was natural because you didn't want some stranger poking around into a subject that was painful enough and you only wanted to put behind you."

"That was it, Philip, nothing more."

"I know. For you anyway. But when I read of the two almost identical murders…"

She interrupted, almost shouting, "Two murders! What are you talking about?"

"The child in Wigstall, in 1951."

"Wigstall? What child? I don't know what you're talking about! Two murders, please tell me it's not true. Stop, I don't want to hear it."

She put her hands over her ears and people in the café stared. A woman at the far end of the café stood up, to see better, sitting down when Philip glared at her.

In fact, Philip was nonplussed. But her astonishment was genuine. So he told her quietly the story of Ann Dexter and the arrest and execution of William Green.

"How terrible. That poor man. And yes, my aunt Hattie's married name was Towles. I have cousins that live in Sheffield. Their name is Towles, too. They're probably related somewhere."

She sighed. "Go on, it's all horrible, but you must go on. I want to hear it all."

"I just felt the two murders had to be connected, even though the police had already hanged someone for the first one. For a long time, I didn't get it, but now I think that all along the police knew that there was something wrong. The murders were too similar, so they knew they must have hanged the wrong man in Green. But they couldn't solve the new one. So they were stuck."

"When I read about Green's trial, I thought it was a bit thin. There's a Professor Tower who is an expert on this. She wrote in a book that there was no real case against him. That fixed it for me, especially after I went down to Hertfordshire to see her.

"At first, I got the idea that Amos Holyroyd had killed them both. He was certainly a good candidate for having killed your sister. If you remember him, he was a terrible, brooding, violent man."

"Yes, I was always scared of him. All of us children were. He would always pop out at you unexpectedly in town and start telling you what a sinner you were. Yes, I can see him as a child molester. Particularly little girls. Oh, no! Boys, more likely! Was he?"

"I don't know. Probably not. Most probably he kept it all bottled up inside. Anyway, that was my idea and when I was knocked on the head, I first thought that John had done that, because I was getting too hot on the trail for his dad. Silly, I know."

"Actually, I was so taken with you I sort of forgot a bit about Wiggy. After all, it was his daughter who was murdered. Not many men would kill their own children.

Molest them, no doubt, but not kill. And there didn't seem to be any connections between Wiggy and Wigstall..."

"Philip..."

"I couldn't see Wiggy clearly, because..."

"Because of me?"

"Well, yes. Then we had dinner – it was the night before last – it was wonderful. I made some silly remark about not minding if the coffee had arsenic in it. Then, in the middle of the night, I thought of arsenic again, and it all fell into place."

"I don't understand."

"Your mother, you see. Why did she die? He killed her, too. Look, I'll start at the beginning. Wiggy was a young footballer who was chosen for the Leicester City development squad or whatever they call it here -- the pool of young talent they sign on straight out of school. So although he had grown up in Cottisthorpe and had no prior connections to any of the people eventually involved, he moved to Leicester.

"I'm guessing that there he fell in with a group of young men, some of whose relatives had moved to the brand-new housing estate out in the suburbs at Wigstall. There they got into various sorts of trouble, and I think it was there that he and one or two of his pals started fooling around with younger and younger girls. One of them, William Green, who like Wiggy was only 15 or so years old, a minor anyway, got caught at it and went to a juvenile home for a while. Once he was out, they started again and Wiggy molested Ann Dexter and something went wrong.

Perhaps he only killed her by mistake. He got away unseen, and the father accused Green. No doubt because of his record. The police arrested Green for the same reason. Easy. He was executed and Wiggy was in the clear."

"Soon his professional career was over, not quite good enough, so he moved back to Cottisthorpe. Perhaps he had known your mother previously. Anyway, he courted her, and they married. He must have been a bit of a character, dashing and brazen. Swept your mother off her feet – I don't know. But he was happy enough to leave Leicester and come here. The new baby came, and things were stable. I can't guess what trouble he was in on the side. But I think he always had this terrible thing for young girls."

He paused awkwardly. If Wiggy had had this problem, Jean, being older than her sister, would surely have felt the brunt of it first. He plunged on.

"I supposed he physically abused your mother, too. Somehow, he had a knack for getting away with things...."

"It's all true." Tears were streaming down her face, and she made no attempt to wipe them away. She sat there, totally bedraggled. It was almost more than he could do not to grab her and hold her tight.

"And it's worse. I tried to interrupt you a minute ago. Aunt Hattie told me that Angela wasn't his baby. He and my mother had separated for a while. Something happened, I don't know. But she was pregnant, and we had to move back."

"So, if Angela was not his child... well, that explains a lot. Angela died and once again Wiggy got away with it. But soon enough someone, the police perhaps, or just some of the men in town, worked it out. I am guessing that Fred Lakin's father knew it. He had family connections in Wigstall, too. They made the connection with the previous murder in Wigstall and saw that with Green executed, Wiggy would be bound to get away with it. At least the first one and perhaps both since there was no evidence.

"And I think your mother worked it out before any of them. Though she may never have said a word, I get the feeling she was too loyal – too scared, perhaps – for her own good. Perhaps she knew his alibi was no good. And who knows, perhaps she told someone.

"Your mother became depressed and sick. Perhaps one day she challenged him. She got that terrible flu that was going around, and it went to her stomach. I'm sorry about this, Jean – I think he poisoned her, to keep her quiet. There was no reason for anyone to die of gastroenteritis in 1962, for heaven's sake. A little rat poison for someone already half-dead with a serious stomach flu, however... too easy. Arsenic, you see?

"It was my mentioning arsenic over dinner that made everything fall into place. I realized, last night. Anyway, once again, no one seemed to suspect Wiggy of anything. There was poor old Wiggy, after all. A bit of a character, not always honest, but good for a laugh in the pub. A double tragedy.

"Whoever it was in town who had worked it out – say it

was Fred's father – eventually decided to take the law into their own hands. A group of them got him one night, warned him off, and then beat him nearly to death, leaving him in the ditch to look like a hit-and-run. I've even been wondering if Amos Holyroyd, the super-righteous Amos, was in that group. He was a violent man. And if his conscience got the better of him later, then perhaps Fred's dad had to take care of him. That's going a bit too far probably, but I'm sure Fred's dad was one of the group that beat up Wiggy.

"That would explain why both Fred and John seemed to know more than they let on, and why they were anxious to keep me away. Another thing that showed me the true story was the man called Towles in the group – he later pretended to "find" Wiggy in the ditch. I think he had second thoughts about it all."

"Yes, I just said. Uncle Ted, Aunt Hattie's husband. They all worked together at Minton's."

"Right. So he definitely knew. Perhaps your mother told her sister and that's who got the group together. I don't know, but ever since, everyone has needed to keep this quiet. A code of silence. A conspiracy of silence for 25 years. Pretty impressive when you think of it. I think John found out somehow – perhaps his father really was involved. And probably the police had a good idea about all of it; they may even have decided to look the other way. Had no choice."

"I thought John was just protecting me."

"Well, he was, in a way."

"Philip, you look pale, and I hate it here. Let's go back over to the hotel."

The walk was painful but not as bad as he expected until the end. The last few hundred yards defeated him. She helped him into and out of the lift and eased him onto the bed.

"Thanks, I'm really wiped out and it hurts again. It'll be better tomorrow."

"Do you have to go to the clinic today?"

"Clean forgot. Never mind."

While he lay back with his eyes closed, she sat on the edge of the bed and started to talk -- about her mother, college, coming back to Cottisthorpe.

"Why did you come back?"

"I don't know. There was a position advertised. I had heard that Wiggy was getting into more and more trouble, and I suppose that deep down I was curious. I would never find out what happened to my sister if I were living down in the South. And I wanted to be near my mother's grave. That's very old-fashioned, I expect. But my father, my real father, had no grave. My mother and little half-sister did."

"And that kept you here."

"Oh, I like it here, it is my home after all. It's a nice town, nice people. I'm happy here."

"You never married."

"Never really wanted to. I didn't trust men and the convent school actually discouraged me from thinking about men. That just made some of the girls more randy, I know. I just never quite got into the way of it. A few boys at Oxford. There were a few boys at Oxford. They all seemed very young. Marriage never came up. I always thought about mum, and Wiggy, and ..."

Philip saw where this might be going and leapt in.

"You're young and beautiful."

"Don't be silly. I'm middle-aged and I was never pretty. Well, John Holyroyd thought I was, once, but he was five years younger than me, and anyway..."

"And..."

"He married someone else. Marian, you've met her. And I was just as glad."

"I think you're beautiful."

She looked at him steadily. "Thank you."

"Speak of the devil." Philip had heard the sound of size fifteen feet on the stairs. Exactly at the wrong – or perhaps it was the right – moment, Holyroyd knocked on the door.

He eyed them suspiciously as if expecting to find evidence of heavy breathing.

"We're getting maudlin in here, John. Come and cheer us up."

"In that case, I've got the right stuff." He produced a bottle of scotch.

"A little celebration. Alright for you, Jean?"

"Why not." She forced a laugh. "Philip's been telling me his wild theories. They don't cast you in an altogether favorable light, either."

John produced three plastic glasses and poured healthy slugs, sitting back-to-front on the rickety chair.

"Whoa, remember it's still not teatime."

"Bugger that! Oh, pardon, Jean. Anyhow, I'm still on duty, and I say, 'Stuff it.' We need a drop of summat."

"John, Philip has told me all about Wiggy and about the other murder, the one in Wigstall, in 1951. He says Wiggy killed them both and the police knew."

There was a heavy silence. Eventually, Holyroyd spoke up.

"I'm sorry Jean, I'm sorry no one told you, but I don't know what good it would have done. And Philip, you're right. When I told my inspector you had been to the library, he told me to warn you off. They didn't want anyone raking over old history that no one could do anything about. We're none too proud of this business; none of us."

"Go on, Philip, tell him the whole lot. Although I think he knows it all anyway. You got it right." Jean had been pacing around the room. Now she sat back on the edge of the bed, holding Philip's hand tightly and fixing him with her dark eyes, which now seemed even larger.

Philip told Holyroyd the whole story, leaving out nothing, even telling him about the first time Wiggy tried to run him down at the allotments. And someone taking the microfiche of the newspapers from the library, the whole story.

"One thing John, I'm sorry. You too Jean. That evening when Jean and I went to the Indian restaurant, someone searched my room while I was out. I thought it was you, but of course it was Wiggy. He had seen us leave together."

"Sounds like Wiggy. And my idea, by the way, is someone from our shoplifted those microfilms, terrible thing to say, ain't it." He laughed.

"And I have to ask this, Jean. Did you follow me to Leicester and to Wigstall, that day? In a blue car? Someone knew I'd been there."

"No, silly! Mine's white, you've seen it. And I lost you that day." She laughed. "I told you I was no good at it. I had parked the car facing the wrong direction. By the time I turned it round, you had gone. It all just shows that you should leave these things to the professionals. The Nottingham library had already called Muriel Henderson to ask about you anyway, and she told John. Small town!"

I'm impressed. In that case, the only other thing I don't understand is this... no, there are two things. First, if I could work all this out, why didn't anyone else before me?"

"That's easy. Anyone might have. But the town had fixed matters in its own way. There was no evidence. Nothing to prosecute with. You never found any real evidence, did you? And it could have turned nasty. In fact, it did turn nasty. We could have had another murder on our hands, yours or someone like you. Then again, Fred's dad, and mine, and Jean's uncle, and a few other blokes had all beaten the shit out of Wiggy. A bloody serious offense. So everyone kept quiet. Except later Fred's dad told him and then Fred told me. But believe me, if there had been any solid evidence, we'd have arrested the old bastard years ago."

"I can see, yes. So my second question may be irrelevant. Why were you all so keen to keep me out of things? What special threat did I represent?"

"Why, you were different; you knew us all. And you were Mr. Clever-Clogs from America with all the degrees and lots of money. People were scared of you. Fred still thinks you're a reporter. Our worst fear was having reporters sniffing around."

"I see. But it's not true. That is, I know you, John, but I didn't know anyone else, not Wiggy, or Fred, or Jean."

"Well, you knew Jean."

"John..." Jean started to speak but Philip interrupted her.

"What?"

"Yes, down on the meadows. Train spotting. She used to come and hang around, too. You and Neil were mad about her."

Philip looked at her. Strung out as she was, her eyes were laughing.

"That was you?"

She just smiled and then leaned forward and kissed him. John Holyroyd looked from one to the other and got up, making sure he still had the bottle. As he closed the door behind him, he observed:

"Reckon I might be in the way here."

And he would have been.

ACKNOWLEDGMENTS

This book would not have been possible without the extraordinary assistance of my daughter, Jessica.

ABOUT THE AUTHOR

Keith Stewart Thomson was Executive Officer of the American Philosophical Society from 2012 – 2017. He is an emeritus professor of natural history at the University of Oxford, former director of the Oxford Museum of Natural History, the Academy of Natural Sciences in Philadelphia, and the Peabody Museum at Yale University where he was also a professor and Dean for many years. He is the author of many books and essays on history, history of science, evolution and paleontology. He currently lives in Gwynned, Pennsylvania with his wife Linda, and their dog Hazel and enjoys visits from his children and grandchildren. *Murder in Cottisthorpe* is his first work of fiction.

Printed in Great Britain
by Amazon